RYE'S REPRIEVE

HARPER RANCH SERIES: BOOK ONE

LOUELLA NELSON

Montana Sky
PUBLISHING

INTRODUCTION

Welcome to Montana Sky Publishing, where authors write books set in my 1880s "world" of Sweetwater Springs and Morgan's Crossing, Montana.

Rye's Reprieve: Harper Ranch Series Book One is written by Louella Nelson. I first met Louella in 1998 when she became my writing teacher, and I joined her critique group. My first book, *Wild Montana Sky*, was written in that group. Since then, Louella has developmentally edited every Montana Sky story. Along the way, we became dear friends. I often go over to her house, and we sit at her dining room table and write. On deadline weeks, I might as well move in with her.

To date, Louella has written four Harper Ranch Series books, with more to come. See a sample of book two, *Rebel Love Song*, at the end of *Rye's Reprieve*.

I hope you enjoy reading *Rye's Reprieve*.

INTRODUCTION

Debra Holland

And ye beneath life's crushing load
Whose forms are bending low,
Who toil along the climbing way
With painful steps and slow,

Look now! For glad and golden hours
Come swiftly on the wing;
Oh, rest beside the weary road,
And hear the angels sing!

—*Rev. Edmund Hamilton Sears (1810-1876)*

Dedicated to Stacee Jo Nelson,
Light of My Life

CHAPTER ONE

Montana Territory, September 23, 1886

Five miles southeast of Morgan's Crossing, near his favorite fishing hole, Rye "Doc" Rawlins saw the biggest goldarn deer ever seen in the West. He leaped from the saddle. Heart racing, he braced his rifle against a crack in a granite boulder and took aim at the patch of dun hide he glimpsed through the cottonwoods and aspens.

He was a lousy shot—had already missed on a ten-point buck two hours ago. This time, steady, steady, he told himself, blocking out the rustle of the river to his right. He drew a breath, held it, slowly let it out, waiting to locate the sweet spot behind the foreleg that would mean a merciful clean kill.

As Rye stared, the animal lifted its head and peered at him. The shape of the head wasn't right, the jaw too heavy, the black nostrils wide and flaring to get his scent. He registered that the animal was a horse, not a deer. A fear-response kicked in—he could be strung up for killing someone's horse—and he shouted, "Ho!"

Simultaneously, out in the choicest fishing hole in this part of Montana rose a water nymph, breasts gleaming beneath a cascade of water. The cool liquid sluiced off a mane of deep-red hair and bared a face and shoulders only Botticelli could paint.

He shouted again in panic, "Ho!"

So the sounds he'd made came out, embarrassingly, "Ho-ho," as if he were humoring children on the eve of Christmas.

The woman, likely in her early twenties, stared at him, eyes in shadow, the pupils no doubt wide in fear, her chest rising in panicked breaths.

His manly parts responded.

Though he was a man of faith, the two events together jolted him as apparitions might were he to find himself alone on a stormy night in an abandoned house.

However, his heart and mind were not to have a reprieve. A second woman of similar age, blond and equally lush, burst out of the deep pool. When she saw Rye, she screamed, sending icicles along his spine.

Then a third appeared, dark-haired and slight, not yet twenty, he guessed. She jumped in fright and clapped her hands over small high breasts, sinking up to her chin to hide herself.

A part of Rye's brain that loved women was at once shocked and thrilled.

But when a last female came up laughing and sputtering, saw him, stared like the first without a scream, Rye glanced away, for she was but a child of thirteen or fourteen.

What to do?

If he mounted his horse, he would have a clear view of the four females, but they would deeply resent him taking their full measure. On t'other side, but for the child it would be a pleasure few men would ever experience and, therefore, not to be missed. He and his mining buddies were short on women in the camp, and these women were beautiful treasures. If he took another look, Reverend Norton, who'd preaching in Morgan's Crossing sometime soon, surely would absolve him. But for the child.

While he debated, one of the women said sternly, "You look again I'll have your eyes in my sights."

Reflexively Rye glanced her way. The redhead. She beaded down on him with a big-bore rifle. Naked, gleaming, and armed. She drew back the bolt with a *snap*. "I said—"

"I'm not, I'm not." He reached for his stud's trailing reins, took a step toward the stirrup.

Metal clicked when she shot the bolt. "Don't you move," she demanded.

He froze.

Water gurgled and splashed; she was no doubt getting out of the pool, reaching for her clothes....

"Missouri?" The high voice of the young girl.

"Get dressed," came the curt response.

Splashing, splashing, murmuring, then silence.

"Look now?" he asked, all politeness. "Ma'am?"

He didn't relish trying to patch a hole in his chest, though he'd done it once on a miner in California who'd lived to tell about it. Neither did he like the target his shoulders and back made.

Slowly he turned. All four were mounted bareback, holding some fine horseflesh with just rope hackamores; a dark-faced foal peeked from the bushes. The redhead was up on the dun mare he'd almost shot. The child rode the biggest red quarter horse he'd every laid eyes on.

He took off his summer straw, ducked his head, said, "Ma'am. Er, ma'ams."

The four of them—the redhead, the blonde, a slender almost boyish gal with her dark hair in a knot, and the girl —all had the same classical features, though only the stunning redhead and the blond sister had voluptuous curves beneath that menswear—dungarees, well-worn cotton shirts, boots. Felt hats in hand. Missouri, the redhead, slipped her hat on and trained the big-bore on him.

He thought he might carry the picture seared in his memory.

The youngster and the one with small breasts looked at each other and smiled. They put on their hats, deepening the charm of the picture—the aspen leaves turning gold around them, the pool reflecting the scene—a perfect Charlie Russell subject.

Though their men's work attire was disconcerting, Rye relaxed a fraction.

"Rye Rawlins," he said. "Of the San Francisco Rawlins. We're in shipping. My father's the mayor. I truly mean you no harm."

"What're you doing snooping around here?" said the redhead as if the place was hers.

"This is my favorite fishing hole and reflecting spot, ma'am."

"Huh. I don't see a pole." She kept the rifle trained but slid a quick look at his horse. "Nice-looking stud."

He nodded. Black Bart, named after the poet-stage robber of San Francisco, was the last remnant of his former comfortable life. The animal was lifting his fine-boned head, stretching his top lip, scenting the mare.

"Looks to have some thoroughbred in him."

Rye stepped toward Bart to pat his withers but the stern voice said, "Stop. Don't you move!"

He paused. "I was going to say, he's a half-brother to Ben Ali."

"The Derby winner?" Apparent surprise made her alto voice rise.

"Yes, ma'am. He's three seasons older, out of a quarter horse dam."

"Quarter, huh?"

"The dam had some Arab in her."

"Accounts for the chiseled head, the big eyes."

"Gave him staying power, too. He can do twenty-five miles without breaking a sweat."

"Huh," she said.

"Missouri," said the child. "I'm hungry."

"Alright, Faelan, hold your horses."

Rye chuckled.

The redhead scowled.

Rye sobered. "You following the river?"

"Why?"

"There's a welcome party tonight in Morgan's Crossing, about five miles downstream. Mrs. Morgan has enticed a friend from St. Louis to run the boarding house. Miss Bertha Bucholtz by name. Everyone's invited."

"Can we?" begged Faelan.

"No."

"Aw, Missouri. We ain't had fun in ages."

Missouri gave her full attention to the girl. "Don't say *ain't*, Faelan. We'll see." To Rye she said, "What time's this party?"

At the thought of interacting more with this woman, he couldn't help the prick to his senses. Old Obadiah might play the fiddle. Surely there'd be dancing. These women would add a mighty boost to the social scene. The miners would go nuts, himself included, but he'd have the inside track. He picked the redhead for himself. He liked a strong woman who made him tow the mark. And he plum liked a western hat on a gal.

"About supper time," he said. He glanced downstream. "Follow the river for a few miles. Cross where the big log has fallen. You'll know it. Stay on the track and cross again at the split rocks and keep coming, or you can head west about two miles, till you see a wagon road. It comes from Sweetwater Springs. Take it to the right. The land drops down some but gentle-like."

"Not that we'll surely come, but thank you, Mr. Rawlins."

He touched the brim of his straw. "The town isn't any Frisco but the people are decent, mostly. We've got several married couples. Plus the new wife, Prudence Morgan from St. Louis. You ladies will be safe. Count on me."

"We'll count on ourselves," she corrected. She lifted the reins, backed the mare. "C'mon, girls."

"Your names?" Rye called.

"Harper. The Missouri Harpers." She touched the mare's flanks, the animal stepped adroitly, and the women and the girl faded into the trees.

Rye felt for a moment that he'd conjured them from dreams or from a novel. And then the longing for the redhead seeped into him and began to make his heart ache.

MINUTES LATER, as they rode toward the wagons, Missouri's heart tripped a wild beat. Although her face was still warm from embarrassment, Rye Rawlins had single-handedly brought the western cowboy into reality. He was the stuff of her dreams—tall, square-jawed, wide of shoulder and narrow of hip, with a ready smile, nice manners, and a fine horse. She imagined him holding her in his strong arms as they waltzed, his warmth bleeding through his cotton shirt and that friendly grin stealing her breath away.

Pure nonsense, she chided. She had a horse farm to build. No time for courting.

"That man was handsome," said Faelan, putting a hand over her heart.

"Beware the handsome fellow," Missouri said. She cut a glance at Susan, riding the bay mare.

Faelan saw it and looked at her hands, gripping the reins. Color came into her cheeks.

Her baby sister was young but wise. They had all suffered for the mistake in judgment Susan had made, being seduced by an unseemly man.

"C'mon, honey," Missouri said. "Let's get some food, then hitch up the horses and mules. We'll want to be in town before the light fades."

"Won't Aunt Gwen be surprised, Missy?"

"I believe she will. We didn't say when we'd arrive."

Faelan rode ahead to chatter with Jessamine, who was riding her favorite, the gray broodmare Dancy. The mare's dappled colt, Traveler, raced about, trotted back, nuzzled its mother, and bounced away. Dancy and Jess were a match: Jessamine's dark hair, set free from its knot, lifted in long lacy tendrils in the breeze, and Dancy's luxurious black tail swept the ground.

Missouri thought, *At least I've made sure my sisters and I are clean and presentable when we meet Aunt Gwenllian.* They'd need to change into dresses to complete the picture of what they were, refined young ladies, although Missouri, at twenty-five, was practically a refined old spinster.

The two Harper brothers, her father and uncle, had had money and married well. Their brides, educated best friends from New York, had remained in contact despite

Uncle William and Aunt Gwenllian "jumping off" to the Montana Territory many years back.

Left to raise her growing family of daughters in the wilderness of Missouri without a best friend near, Mama Harper had carried on her high standards for etiquette, generosity to others, and a sense of fairness. She had inspired in her girls a belief in "the values, rights, and privileges due all citizens, equally, in the glorious American republic."

Missouri chuckled in appreciation at the memories. "Women must not subjugate themselves to men's wills," Mama had insisted many times. Though she was a Presbyterian, all her life Mama would be influenced by the suffragette activities of her younger years. Marriage was to be a partnership, not a dictatorship. She had taught the girls that appearances and self-respect counted; that they should improve themselves as far as was possible in life and not leave the difficult business of running things to the men.

"Cleanliness," her mother had always said, "was next to godliness. However, an egalitarian spirit and strength of character hold sway over all."

Missouri's heart pinched at the loss of her mother.

And she missed her Papa, too. His hard work and his open-mindedness in regard to women's roles had seen Missouri through college and a veterinarian degree from Cornell when it just wasn't done; Susan through two years of study in music and drawing, though she was widely read on agriculture; and Jessamine through to a degree in the Classics that would provide depth to her writing. And Faelan, well, Mama had seen to it her youngest child had a fine background in the basics until Mama and Papa's tragic deaths last fall.

Though Missouri longed for her mother, she supposed

due to her medical training she was more pragmatic than most women and did not dwell on tragedy. After all, there was far too much to do in life.

With visions of a soft feather bed, elegant meals, and refined conversation urging her toward her aunt's ranch, situated across the creek from Morgan's Crossing, she nudged her mount, and the four young women left the trees.

They moved at a trot toward two wagons covered by canvas bonnets, sheltering beneath the shade of granite outcroppings set amid the golden prairie. Night-winds swept these rolling hills at high elevation, chilling them till their lips were blue. After months of overland travel, her aunt's fine home was looking better and better.

Their farm animals grazed on sparse grasses near their foreman, Rio, who was leaning against a wagon, repairing harness, and their chickens scratched underfoot. When Rio saw the girls riding in, he began to scoop up his feathered friends. Two wagons comprised their worldly goods and the seeds of their future life, along with two mules, two Percherons, four riding horses of good stock, a spring colt, Rio's mustang, the chickens, Faelan's cat, and Stowe the cow, named after their mother's author friend.

Missouri's heart swelled to know they'd come this far without losing anything but a chicken, and that to a two-legged thief in the caravan they'd left behind in Miles City.

AFTER A COLD DINNER OF BEANS, cornbread, and smoked venison, they set the work horses and mules into their traces and saddled up. The girls dressed like men and rode like men, their best camouflage. Missouri rode the dun mare alongside Jessamine's Dancy and Faelan's big red gelding Moses, while Susan took her turn driving the wagon drawn by the mules, her saddle horse tied behind. Trailed by his mustang, Rio drove the other wagon, his hands tanned mahogany from months of driving, his face set to possible danger.

Though he seemed ageless, Rio was forty-four, a *vaquero* with no last name and no past, originally from New Mexico Territory and her late-father's overseer. He was taciturn, whipcord strong, and savvy about everything from foaling to water systems, crops, repairs, and provisioning. He was a crack shot and had brought the sisters venison, rabbit, beaver, and elk on the trip west.

Most of all he was a trusted friend willing to work without wages on the journey and for the initial years it would take to prove-up the homestead acres she and Susan had purchased. Missouri had told Rio she could not pay him a wage, giving him a chance to find another job.

At her talk of wages, Rio had not answered her. He had simply gone to the barn and begun outfitting the mules and Percherons with harnesses sturdy enough for four months of travel across scorched plains, swift streams, mud holes, and mountain passes.

Although Rio would never acknowledge the deep affection the Harper girls felt for him, Missy sensed the affection was returned. There seemed to be no apparent joy in him. But his gentleness with the creatures and an unequalled diligence made the Harpers forgive his secret heart and feel grateful beyond words he was with them.

Still following the watercourse, they circled flat-topped buttes, keeping well away from the thick stands of hardwoods, pines, and willows crowding the waterway. Entering from the east, they came into a small valley. Missouri hoped this was Morgan's Valley, where the town lay, but was disappointed to see no habitation but a coyote traveling across the fall prairie grass.

The mountains to the south fell further into the distance, purple with haze. They wound through a series of meadows divided by ridges of rock and cactus, the water, far below, rushing and slowing by turns. Keeping to the track others had trod before them, including Rye Rawlins and his magnificent horse, they crossed and re-crossed the river and dry creek beds, and even a few streams still flowing, with rills that fed the bigger stream.

At every step, the sun pelted down. Missouri lifted her wide-brimmed felt hat, fanned her face. She glanced at Rio.

He seemed not to suffer in the heat the way she and her sisters did. Brown face set, he never relented sweeping his gaze across the arroyos, the gulches, the rocks that could hide rattlesnakes, the foothills rising into a blue-gray range of mountains ahead to the northwest. In a high gulch, a cabin nestled among the pines, no smoke rising.

Lonesome and primitive, Missouri thought, and was glad of her family.

She wondered about Rio's thoughts. Was he reminded of his home somewhere in New Mexico Territory? Would he love this new land? Or miss the green of her home state? Would she?

Their caravan had followed the curving water for the time it took to eat up four or five miles pulling two wagons, and now the water bent west toward the hazy mountains.

They rounded a bend and a pretty valley opened up.

"Look, Missy," called Faelan, and they all held their breath for a moment. "Is that it? Are we almost there?"

Unfortunately, they were not. Nary a cabin nor general store in sight. "Soon, pet, soon," soothed Missouri. "Remember that cowboy said five miles."

"Oh, Jess," cried the fourteen-year-old. "We're almost to heaven."

"Don't blaspheme, sweet one," said Jessamine, fluffing the front of her plaid men's shirt to let out the heat. But she was smiling. "We'll have fine food and a feather bed tonight, I'll warrant."

"But we shall go to the party first," Faelan insisted, face aglow. "Missy said."

The sisters chuckled indulgently. Her baby sister only expressed what they all felt.

Missouri was saddle-weary, sunburned, and tired of living in a tent, the responsibility of seeing to the safety of her younger sisters constantly in her mind. The girls were just as tired of the journey and eager for community as she was. Community meant less fear for them all. She had enjoyed their great adventure, true enough; but she was also hungry for the safety of four solid walls and protection from predators of every stripe.

Anticipation riffled through her. Missouri hadn't told the westerner they had been headed for Morgan's Crossing all along. The four months traveling through the Territories had made her cautious of men—and she hadn't mentioned they were intending to beg shelter from their aunt and live in the comfort of the ranch house—a veritable mansion, according to Auntie's letters of years gone by. Hopefully there was room in the barn for at least the broodmares until she and Rio could gauge the safety of the valley.

Though Missouri kept an eye out for wolves and hostiles as the wagons edged around the base of another ridge, the notion of seeing Mr. Rawlins in company played at the edges of her thoughts.

Would the Morgan couple believe in music and dancing? She fancied a lively reel or a waltz. What woman didn't? Despite her keen focus on the horse farm and a kind of grinding self-discipline, she was always glad for a turn with a fine-looking gentleman.

What did her aunt think of this man Rye Rawlins of the San Francisco Rawlins? Would it be fitting to dance with him? Even so, Missouri could make up her own mind. Mr. Rawlins had been a gentleman, after all, calling out a warning rather than hide in the bushes and stare his fill. She'd seen warmth in his eyes but not lasciviousness.

Before she could speculate more on the dancing, she felt pity. Her aunt would be serving with the other widows, not dancing with her husband. Missouri had heard mining was a dangerous business, so surely there were other women of a similar situation to befriend her. She hoped her aunt fared well, but if she were blue with heartache, she would at least have four lively young women to cheer her.

And Auntie would cheer them. Soon Missouri and her sisters would rest on fine upholstered furniture and bask in the wealth of their only remaining family.

Wealth, Aunt Gwenllian had written eight or nine years ago. Then she and Uncle William had spent years making a go of the 160-acre cattle ranch they'd bought from a former owner. That news—an unknown venture for the couple, on a relatively small piece of land for a ranch--had concerned Missouri's father, who, years ago, had served one half of his fractured country and multiplied his own wealth, raising horses for the Union Army. After worrying the family, sometime later Aunt Gwen had written that their fortune had been "improved" by Mr. Morgan's mining operation and the beneficence of the Lord, and Papa had been somewhat mollified.

Missouri remembered the many family discussions around the supper table. Her aunt and uncle had been the heroes of her own secret dreams of adventure. *Now we're following in their footsteps.*

Improved. What had Aunt Gwen meant?

"Missy," said Faelan, riding over. "Jess and I have decided we'll hope for Aunt Gwen's raspberry jam on hot biscuits."

"For breakfast or at the social?" she asked, amused.

"At the party, silly," said Faelan. "What'll you hope for?"

"I'll say…" She held her breath. *So hard to choose.*

"What, what?" asked Faelan.

"Her blueberry tarts," said Missouri, laughing. She was nearly weak with anticipation of those delights.

Aunt Gwen's letters had often tantalized her eager readers with details of her compotes and preserves: apple, plum, raspberry, black currant. Her neighbors, claimed Auntie, were fond of her prickly pear jam and her blueberry tarts. Missouri's mouth watered.

What else might be had at the Morgans' party? This occupied the conversation as the schooners followed the water downstream.

At last the path bent northwest, edged on the far bank by a barbed-wire fence that wove through the willows. The bark on the stems within reach had been stripped by hungry cattle.

The land opened into a great valley of rolling hills, the grasses turned golden by dry winds. The prairie rose in the distance to hills studded with rocks and stubby pines, and beyond, thick forest, the sheer faces of red rock, and then the mountains. And over all, a cloudless dome that was the deepest blue Missouri had ever seen. It was a big place, sweeping, majestic.

But when Missouri's heart quickened in eagerness, she warned herself of the struggle to survive that lay ahead.

In this arid land, she would need to irrigate to grow wheat or even a kitchen garden, and was glad of the water that edged their acres. She was near breathless to see their homestead for the first time, to see what was needed and what would sustain them.

Faelan leaned over to pat the neck of her seventeen-hand sorrel gelding Moses. "We're almost there," she reassured him.

Moses nodded onward, his lower lip flapping like an elderly steed's, though he was only five, the quickest quarter horse at roundups and the gentlest beast in their stable.

Their father had bought the colt unseen from the King Ranch in Texas, hoping for new blood for his own brand. But Moses didn't have the conformation her father was looking for, so he'd gelded the colt and trained him to cut horses from the *remuda*. It would be at least two years before Traveler could be bred, and Missouri was without a stallion as she tried to establish a horse ranch. Traveler's sire, a well-known and respected stallion, had been killed in the same storm that had taken her parents.

She thought again of Mr. Rawlins' stud and wondered if they could come to some kind of arrangement....

While she was musing about her horses, cattle appeared on the hills. They passed telegraph poles. There were ranches on her left now.

They came up out of a depression and climbed one more hill.

Missouri glanced up. Through the trees, they glimpsed a well-trodden wagon road to their left, running parallel to their approach and just this side of the river. A railed bridge ahead spanned the water as it flowed northwest, and beyond, another smaller stream looked as if it intersected like an *X* with the main river, this one flowing northeast.

"Missy, a town!"

"Yes, pet. I see it. We're here at last."

Sure enough, backlit by the lowering sun and snug-set between the two waterways, a straggle of wooden buildings rose into the gloaming. Sharp-pointed shadows reached out from the structures toward the approaching caravan.

"It don't look like much," said Faelan, an edge of excitement nonetheless making her tone high.

"*Doesn't,*" corrected Missouri, struck by a pang of foreboding.

"Some don't make a show of their wealth," said Jessamine, sounding brave but disappointed.

"At least we'll have a real bed," said Susan, flicking the mules' driving reins.

"*Ándale, mijas,*" said Rio, snapping his own reins—his way of expressing eagerness, Missouri supposed. The Percherons, Betsy and Vesta, nodded to one another and plodded on.

Had they come the wrong way? Was this scrap of village the town? Missouri squinted to her left, where the road forked after the bridge, and saw at least one two-story structure, gray with burgundy trim and a nice white porch. Perhaps that was the Harper ranch house? *Let it be.*

No, no, she corrected. The barn was too small, and the house had no acreage.

Missouri rose in her stirrups to have a better look at the area. Aligned to the right of the gray home—a few shacks, a second two-story with a false front, a couple of other buildings, more cabins, some tents. In the other direction, the fork led a winding way out of town and disappeared around the shoulder of a bulky mountain.

Across the water from town, on the outside curve of

the smaller stream, lay pale buildings with missing windows and a briar of broken fences. *The Harper Ranch?* Missouri's stomach clutched. *It couldn't be.* And yet the place stood exactly where Auntie had written it would be.

When they came closer to the village, they crossed the main river at a wide spot, and the trail began to follow the stream. They arrived at a humble crossroads: a plank bridge on the left gave access to the town, and on the right, a wagon path followed the chief waterway west, its left bank edged with bits of fencing that stretched into the distance. What was left of Harper fencing, no doubt.

As Missouri's group kept going toward the ranch, they saw people in town walking about, mostly men, hair slicked back or bound, shirts tucked, boots shined, the populace evidently heading toward the social. Missouri searched for Mr. Rawlins but didn't see him.

The townsfolk stopped and stared. Some pointed.

Faelan waved, Susan looked away, and Missouri and Jess nodded, even while their party kept following the lesser stream, driving beneath a canopy of old oaks, pine, and cottonwoods, where the air cooled their cheeks.

The wheels of the wagons creaked and the harness jingled, sounds familiar to Missouri yet heightened by emotions coursing through her.

One feeling was dread.

Another was a strange insistent longing to see the western stranger.

CHAPTER TWO

Something was missing and Rye was worried.

At the Meeting Hall, the party was raucous and merry, the guests jabbering, cutlery clinking, the tables lining one long wall decorated with greenery and laden with delectable foods.

Rye had eaten one of Widow Harper's blueberry tarts, two legs of fried chicken brought over by Mrs. Copelin, three pickled sage-hen's eggs, a huge chunk of cornbread slathered in Mrs. Tuccio's sweet butter, and a couple of forkfuls from a jar of smoked trout he'd contributed. He was plumb full and was topping it all off with a jelly glass brimming with home-brewed beer, tangy with a hint of spruce oil.

The missing element was the four Harper gals. They were late.

Over by the small stove, folded into the bentwood chair that always looked too small for him, red-nosed Obadiah Kettering tuned his violin.

Rye sauntered over. He tilted his libation at him. "Obadiah," he said, nodding.

"Doc," said the man.

Rye winced inwardly at the nickname, but he didn't object.

Adjusting the tension on the strings, the violinist ogled Rye's glass of beer.

Two miners flanked the man, arms folded, looking serious.

"On guard, are you fellers?" Rye asked, grinning.

"Yep," said one—Jeeters by name—a man as tall as Obadiah but built with more muscle.

The other, hair like a snowfield, kept his silence and his military bearing. Rye knew him to be an old Reb, who still ate with his knife.

"Heard Morgan threatened to throw Obadiah in the river if he took a drink tonight," Rye said to Jeeters, making conversation while he looked toward the door, hoping to see the lovely Harper ladies.

Jeeters said, "Can't have our Obie tossing up his dinner on another of Mrs. Morgan's frocks."

Obadiah gave the two of them an owlish look.

This wasn't going to be easy for Obie, watching the town imbibe spirits and beer when he couldn't touch a drop. Somebody had set a Mason jar of river water near the chair-leg, but a stubborn streak wouldn't allow the musician to drink it.

In August, the fiddler had scandalized Prudence Morgan by regurgitating the contents of his stomach onto the skirts of her ocean-blue evening gown. So tonight Mr. Morgan had set guards on the man to keep him from "the demon rum."

Rye glanced toward the new bride. All the woman's beauty was in her bearing. Something about her had softened since getting hitched to Morgan. He couldn't figure out what. Certainly not her backbone. Tall and dressed in her finery, she looked as though she could conduct a war campaign. Several women from Sweetwater Springs floated around Mrs. Morgan; comely butterflies, their husbands huddling nearby, deep in conversation about crops and the weather. The only single female was plump, shy Bertha Bucholtz, the woman of the hour.

"Nice to see some comely ladies tonight," said Rye.

"Dresses us up some, don't it?" said Jeeters. "Too bad there ain't enough single ones to dance with."

"Night's not over yet," said Rye, keeping it mysterious. "I'll see you a bit later, gentlemen."

"Ain't no gentleman," argued Jeeters.

"Speak for yourself," groused Obadiah, who knew many classical pieces and had performed in San Francisco.

Rye wandered off. He kept an eye on the door. *Where was that beautiful redhead?*

Now that his belly was full and he could think straight, Rye realized Miss Missouri Harper had tried to hornswoggle him. Why, the Harper females had been headed for Morgan's Crossing all along. The Widow Harper and the young women he'd met at the river this morning were kin. Had to be. Not that the widow had bothered to tell him her nieces were coming to town, and that there were four of them, all beauties. No, all he'd heard the past year or so was about the tragic deaths of the widow's brother-in-law and his wife, her dearest friend.

He supposed that broken-down ranch across the stream was where the sisters were headed.

Missouri Harper's subterfuge amused him, and yet he understood. She had a huge responsibility riding on her shoulders—the protection of her sisters and, if he figured right, all they owned in a wagon he hadn't yet seen. No outsider would be allowed into that inner circle. As well it should be.

On the off chance the ladies' arrival was to be a surprise, he'd kept his mouth shut, not saying aught to the widow. He'd already said how fine her tarts were and had asked after her health—surreptitiously checking to see if she looked headachy or over-tired. She did. Her cheeks were bright, a sign her blood pressure was elevated. He hoped she was taking the herbs he'd given her.

If the Harper girls were coming to see their aunt—and most certainly they were—where were they? Had they come to harm?

Maybe he ought to saddle Black Bart and go have a look-see. He'd need a lantern, his rifle, and a bedroll, just in case....

RIO CLIMBED down from the wagon box to stand beside Missouri, who was staring dumbstruck at the ranch house, her stomach in knots.

Jessamine and Susan had locked arms and were huddled as if in pain.

Faelan had buried her face in the fur of her tabby cat, and was murmuring, "Don't be upset, Cowboy. It's going to turn out alright...."

Missouri tore her gaze from the eyesore that was her late-uncle's ranch house, with its loose siding, sagging porch, and broken window, and glanced at Rio to see his reaction.

"*Tenemos mucho trabajo en los próximos años,*" he said, sounding matter-of-fact.

"*Si,*" said Missouri, feeling the dread of all the years of work ahead of them. "*Mucho.*"

She couldn't believe the rough shape of the house, although all but the paint on the four-door bunkhouse and the mammoth barn seemed to have survived the gale-force winds and driving sleet that she'd heard characterized the winters in Montana Territory.

"The sign over the gate said Harper Ranch," said Susan, "but I can scarce believe it's—"

"The place we've risked all to come to," finished Jessamine, looking defeated.

"It's not lived in," said Missouri, concerned. "At least not by humans. Where is Aunt Gwen?"

"I hope she's alright," said Susan.

"We'll go to town and find out," said Missouri.

They stood stone-silent for a long minute, staring. The moment stretched out, until—

"*Bueno*," said Rio. "*Vamos a trabajar.*"

"Yes," Missouri sighed. "Let's go to work. Rio, see if the barn is safe, will you?"

"*Si.*" He strode off.

"Girls, you want to tie off the horses to that hitching post—" she gestured to a structure of graying logs "—and check out the house with me?"

"I do," said Faelan, heading for the porch.

"Be careful," called Missouri. "Wait for us."

In an hour or so, the sun would dip behind the mountains that rose behind the valley. With the day fading, they needed to at least unload the trunks to find garments suitable for a party in town—*no, not town. Camp.* Morgan's Crossing looked to be little more than a mining camp. Across the creek, in one of those buildings or tents, she hoped to find her aunt.

But first she'd make sure nobody was going to fall through the stairs and get hurt in this "mansion" they'd expected to call home.

❧

WHEN RYE WENT OUTDOORS, a knot of miners stood on the road, gesturing and talking, their focus on the goings-on across the stream. Through a break in the trees, Rye could see two prairie schooners in the ranch yard, and someone was driving two sets of horses away from the rigs toward the barn. That activity told Rye he didn't need a bedroll but maybe a lantern, and he'd see if he could lend a hand—hurry the arrival process so he could have that dance with Missouri Harper.

He headed off to his cabin to use the privy and saddle Bart.

Relief was a fine thing, he thought minutes later, tightening the braided-rope cinch hugging Bart's belly. Being always eager for adventure, his buddy never bloated or was stubborn on purpose as some horses were, and the gear went on in a jiffy.

In the last warmth of the day, he made his way across the plank bridge, took a left, crossed by a downed section of fence, wound along the river trail, and drew up to assess the situation.

The house was fifty yards or so away on a low plateau, safe from spring floods. The gate stood without fencing, made of unhewn, weathered pine logs reaching into the dusky-pink sky. Above, a plank with *Harper Ranch* burned into it hung crookedly on frayed ropes strung between the two poles. Attached to one of the post uprights was an old chute and ramp for loading cattle.

Up at the house, someone carried a bundle from one of the wagons and hurried inside.

At one time the place would have been a fine home, but now it was bleached and broken, like the fences. It was a two-story place with a porch that ran maybe forty or fifty feet. At the far end, a rail was splintered and sagged out of line. He could fix that in two shakes of a cow's tail.

A skeleton of wood boards set on a round stone-and-masonry base was probably the well or maybe a spring that had lost most of its housing. What looked to be a sizeable garden overgrown with weeds and a meager orchard separated the main house from a low bunkhouse with several doors. Across a large open space rose great bleached barn. Above the upper-story hay door, the hay hook looked like a rusted spider.

Missouri and her sisters were going to have their hands full making a go of this place. They'd surely need help.

He heard a horse nicker to his left, near the creek, and rode that way. He came through the trees to a half-circle of gravel bank that sloped conveniently to the water.

There stood the young one—Faelan, he recalled—surrounded by the unsaddled saddle horses, who looked up at him, judged him no enemy, and put their heads back down to suck in the cool water. The colt he'd seen back at the river, head and shoulders midnight black and rump speckled like a robin's egg, gave a squealing whinny.

When Bart didn't answer, the youngster drank again.

"Hello, Mr. Rawlins," said Faelan, smiling. She gestured with the rope leads toward town.

Some distance away, the Meeting Hall windows were lit for the welcome party for Miss Bucholtz, and men clustered at the side of the building to smoke and jaw.

"Have you been to the party?" she asked.

"I have, Miss Harper."

"And was it splendid?"

"Yes, it was. The candles are throwing a warm light. The food is fine, and the music is about to start."

"Oh, dancing! I adore dancing, don't you?"

"Well, I do if I have a pretty lass like you to whirl around."

She blushed charmingly. "How you talk, sir. I never."

He chuckled. "Your aunt--" he made a guess at the relationship "--brought the most delicious blueberry tarts."

"Oh, the blueberry! Missy will be so pleased."

So the widow was their aunt, as he'd suspected. "Miss Missouri likes blueberries, does she?"

"Yes, indeed. She's wild for blueberries."

He locked that away for future reference.

Bart stepped near the rump of Missouri's dun, and the mare squealed a warning. Rye backed the stud off.

Faelan gave the mare a soothing pat. "My aunt is a whiz at making preserves, so I'm told. What's your favorite, Mr. Rawlins?"

"Why, I guess I'm partial to peach. Although currant is refreshing in the morning."

"I prefer raspberry, or at least I think I do. I've never tasted Aunt Gwen's raspberry preserves, you see. I was a babe-in-arms when she jumped off for the Territory."

Rye preferred not to explain that he'd jumped off as well. It always gave him an ache to remember why.

When the horses had drunk their fill, he backed his mount so Faelan could get the horses started to the ranch. The sky was a blaze of orange and magenta, tinting the weathered wood structures and the valley grasses.

When they got to the yard, a lantern glowed down at the barn. Not a soul was in sight anywhere. But he heard women's voices indoors.

"I'll tell Missy you're here," offered Faelan, flipping the ropes over the hitching rail and dashing inside.

The foal began to nurse at the gray mare.

"Missy!" Faelan yelled. "You've got a gentleman caller."

Hmm. How did she know he wanted to see Missouri? That girl was a wonder. So much like another child, lost to him now. The thought of her weighed on him.

Rye tied Bart off on a bush a few yards from the Harper horses so the stud would cause no trouble and went toward the two porch steps.

Before he could get there, Missouri appeared and crossed to the post, her face registering surprise. She wore a gown of light green silk, fitted around her full bosom and narrow waist and then falling in lush folds to the floorboards.

He backed away, staggered, for he was struck dumb by her beauty. His memory filled in the hidden curves and the smooth alabaster of her skin. All that showed now were her tanned hands and face, a sculpted face with refined classical features tinted rose by the color of the light. Her hair rippled in a shining mass past her shoulders, catching all the sunset God had ever provided for man's pleasure.

The strains of Obadiah's violin floated over the rustle of the north-flowing stream, a mockingbird whistled, and Rye Rawlins fell in love with Missouri Harper.

Startled by the sudden appearance of the man who'd been in her thoughts so much today, Missouri felt heat flood her cheeks.

He was clean-shaven and handsome in his off-white shirt and black leather vest.

"Mr. Rawlins?" Missouri asked, but gently, for she was very sure he was lost in some kind of reverie. She was blushing madly, which nonplussed her. "Mr. Rawlins, why are you here?"

"Missouri Harper, you are the prettiest, most stunning—"

"Mr. Rawlins," she said, embarrassed for the second time that day.

He appeared to shake himself awake. "What? Beg pardon, Miss Harper."

"Is everything alright?" She glanced across the waterway. "Is my aunt——?"

"Mrs. Harper is fine. That is——" He appeared to collect his wits, and he said, "She could do with a few months of loving care, but I believe her to be as well as can be expected."

"Why, what do you mean? I expect her to be quite well."

"For her age, Miss Harper, but she has had a time of it, losing William—your uncle?—and fending alone."

"She's at the party?"

He nodded.

So Auntie was doing poorly. But the news that her aunt was attending the social event relieved Missouri, for she had feared the worst when she hadn't found her aunt at home. Gwenllian's poor health explained so much about the condition of the ranch.

"I will go to her in just a while, and you'll have no more worries about her care."

He smiled but said nothing, holding her gaze. His eyes were blue, and a shiver touched her. She was glad of the sunset to hide her blushes. "We'll get Faelan dressed and be off, then."

He glanced at the wagons, still bursting with goods. "May I be of any help to you?"

"We thought it best to save most of the unloading for the morning. We'll have to make a few repairs before moving things in." She glanced at her horses. "Rio, our foreman, took the cow and the work animals to the barn. I'd be grateful if you'd bring him our riding horses. They've got to be powerfully hungry."

Missouri hadn't yet worked up the courage to ask if she could put Mr. Rawlins' stud with the mares next spring, or what he would charge in stud fees.

She glanced at him. He wore a black felt Western-style hat whose brim echoed the firm line of his jaw. She was about to speak when—

"Here on the left is your Aunt Gwenllian's place," he said. He stopped, raised the lantern to show a humble cabin with a single chimney and a fenced garden with dried blooms near a shallow porch.

"Oh, my…." She couldn't keep the dismay from her voice.

"Mr. Rawlins," said Faelan, absently fluffing her corduroy skirts, "you must be mistaken. Auntie is a wealthy lady. She'd never live here."

He frowned.

Missouri gazed at Mr. Rawlins. Stabbed with pity for her poor aunt, in a lowered voice she asked, "You're speaking the truth, aren't you?"

"The cabins are really not so bad. We've got neighbors close by to call upon if a need arises."

"We?"

He turned, glanced across the road. "My place."

She saw rocks and scrub brush artfully arranged in the dry front yard and along both sides of the cabin. A filigree of branches rose above the roof from the far side.

"I've got a small corral back there and a shelter for hay and two horses. I'll put Bart up and be right back to take you to the hall."

Apparently the Morgans were hosting there.

Mr. Rawlins returned presently, and they began walking again.

Someone came out of the last cabin on the right. He was a big man, hair parted in the middle and slicked down, bushy beard, homespun shirt clean but worn, suspenders holding his britches in place. The fellow came whistling to his gate, a fancy wrought-iron indulgence, opened it, stepped into the road, closed it, and stopped in his tracks. He quit whistling.

"Rawlins," he said on a high note. "Who have you got there?" His gaze lingered on Jessamine's face.

"The Misses Harper," Mr. Rawlins said, raising the lantern. "Kin to Will's wife."

"Oh, Will." The fellow ran a large hand over his face as if to wipe away a shadow.

"Misses Harper, meet my good friend Mr. Bethesda Janes."

Beth Jane, thought Missouri. *Poor man.*

She, Faelan, and Susan curtseyed. Jess ducked her head. One didn't curtsy in menswear.

Mr. Janes bobbed toward each of them in turn, like a duck bobbing for worms, and his gaze held for a moment on Jess. He said to Mr. Rawlins, "You goin' to the shindig?"

"Been and gone. Coming back for seconds. These ladies need to meet their relative, so…."

Missouri snugged her shawl around her. Mr. Rawlins offered his arm, which, liking the gesture, she accepted, and they began to walk.

Mr. Janes fell into step beside him, both men shortening their strides for the sake of the ladies.

Susan and Jess came next, arm in arm. Missouri glanced over her shoulder to see Faelan twirl once and come in behind them, quiet in the presence of the immense stranger.

Pride swept over Missouri. With Mama and Papa gone, this was her family now, the girls and their auntie. She prayed she could keep them all safe.

and, grateful, she took the trembling fingers of Jess and Faelan in her own cool grip.

"Where is Auntie?" asked Faelan. Her eyes, a striking amber, were lit with excitement. "Look, Missy. The food. So very much...."

Missouri hugged Faelan and searched the mob of people. *There, arranging the plates of food...was that...?*

Oh, Auntie, she lamented. Petite Gwenllian was rail-thin, and her old-fashioned mourning gown was oft-mended. Her hair was snowy, her face lined, too lined for age forty-five. "Come, Faelan, I see her. Sisters—" she glanced at her tiny entourage "—your best manners. Make Mama proud."

They started for the tables of food. But Mr. Rawlins and his friends were suddenly in the way. She must beard the lions first, then.

"Mr. and Mrs. Morgan, may I present the Misses Harper?" Mr. Rawlins completed refined introductions, his manners admirable.

Mr. Morgan said he hoped they enjoyed the party.

Mrs. Morgan extended a gloved hand to each of the Harper women. "Welcome to our town," she intoned, all politeness. "I understand you are the nieces of Mrs. Harper and her late husband. My condolences."

Missouri didn't know if she meant because of her aunt's poor straights or the death of their uncle.

"Thank you," Missouri murmured. "I hope I may call upon you one day soon to get acquainted?"

"Of course. You must meet my houseguests. Come for tea at three o'clock tomorrow."

The invitation was a directive. Missouri nodded and said softly, "Yes, tomorrow, then. But right now, I must go to our aunt. I'm afraid our presence will be a shock for her. She doesn't expect us." She turned.

Aunt Gwen caught sight of her and dropped the serving spoon with a clatter. She gripped the table edge, her face gone pale.

Missouri muttered an apology and hurried to Gwenllian's side, taking her arm. "Aunt. I'm your niece, Missouri Harper."

"I thought—thought you were Adelaide. A ghost—"

"No, aunt," she said, leading her shocked relative to a chair at the end of the table. "I'm—we're her children. Mama—that is, I am Mama's eldest." She gestured, "And this is Susan."

Susan curtsied.

"This is Jessamine."

Jess inclined her head.

"Here is our baby sister, Faelan."

Faelan stepped forward, curtsied, and said in a rush, "They call me that, but I'm not a baby, though I was when I met you once."

"You've certainly gown, child."

"Aunt Gwenllian, we are all so very pleased to meet you again. Mr. Rawlins said you brought your blueberry tarts. Those are Missouri's favorite. Mr. Rawlins says they are very fine. I believe I would like your raspberry, but I'm not certain, for I imagine your blueberry are wonderfully light and delicious. I—"

"Mr. Rawlins," said Gwen barely above a whisper. "Yes, my friend Rye Rawlins. He's kind to me."

First name basis, Missouri noticed. *My friend.*

Aunt Gwenllian raised faded blue eyes to Missouri. "So like your mother, child. Mr. Harper was happy at the match when your father married my best friend. We were close, you know, your mother and I. Marched in New York for women's rights and abolition."

Susan stepped forward, gently touching their aunt's thin shoulder. "Have you eaten tonight, Aunt Gwenllian?"

The tired gaze swept to Susan, ran down her buxom figure, clad in the cornflower gown that matched her eyes. "Jessamine?"

"No, Aunt. Susan. Mama's second daughter. I'm twenty-one. May I get you a plate? A cup of punch?"

"All right, child. I've forgotten to eat. I was helping Mrs. Rivera, Mrs. Tisdale, and the other ladies make the hall suitable for a ball." She chuckled. "Well, not a ball, really, for we are not in the city, are we?"

Missouri knew she meant New York City, a far-away exotic place where her own parents had met and fallen in love—a luxury she herself might never possess.

The violin played a lovely tune. Couples took the floor and began to sway, and Susan left to get a plate of food. Missouri and her sisters were practically faint with hunger, but there would be time to eat after they saw to Aunt Gwen's needs.

"Are you staying at the Morgans'?" their aunt asked.

"No, dear, at the ranch," said Missouri. "I hope you don't mind?"

"The ranch! But that's impossible. You all look so elegant. I've left most of the furnishings but that old place is a wreck. My cabin has just one room. You must stay somewhere befitting your—oh my, such a small town... can't stay at the boarding house—too filthy...."

She was making herself upset.

"Aunt Gwen," said Faelan, sending an encouraging grin toward her aging relative. "We had the most marvelous adventures this summer. We'll tell you all about them, all right? I have a tabby cat. His name is Cowboy. He's had an adventure, too. He nearly got eaten by a red fox, but I snatched him clean away from its jaws, Rio shot it, and now Cowboy sleeps on its pelt."

"Faelan," urged Missouri, "perhaps wait till Aunt has eaten."

"Nonsense," said her aunt. "I've waited years to hear your stories, and I'll hear every one. Only where will you stay, three well-bred ladies—" she glanced at slender Jessamine, took in the trousers and men's shirt "—three ladies or four?"

"Four, ma'am," said Jessamine. "I dress like this because I've gotten used to it. And dungarees are actually much more comfortable than dresses."

"It's unseemly," said Aunt Gwen.

Jess looked abashed.

"But that's all right. Britches are a sign of power in our time, my dear. Yes, you'll get some criticism, but don't pay it any mind. Be true to your nature. Be strong. Be stronger than I was—"

Again she broke off, and Missouri was grateful when Susan brought the food and cup of punch.

"There now, Auntie, eat your fill," murmured Susan, tucking a napkin under Gwenllian's chin. "I'll go and get another plate so you don't have to eat alone."

"Faelan, Jess, go with your sister," said Missouri. "I'll stay with our aunt."

"Come, girls," said Susan.

Across the room, Mr. Rawlins stood watching, and when their gazes met, Missouri felt a strong tug within.

CHAPTER THREE

Bethesda Janes was a brave man, Missouri thought. He'd waited till Jessamine had eaten, and then, undeterred by her male attire, had asked her to dance. They were out on the floor now, causing people to stare. The big man was surprisingly adept at the two-step, Jess looking tiny in his arms—an odd couple with a glow on their faces.

It made Missouri ache to see Jess happy after the travails of the past year.

Wondering how long it would take Mr. Rawlins to ask her to dance—she hoped he'd eventually want to recapture the attraction he'd displayed at the ranch--she at last felt released enough from responsibilities to eat something.

Excusing herself from Susan and Aunt Gwen, who were deep into a discussion about raspberry-picking, and casting a quick glance to check on nearby Faelan, who was watching the dancers and mimicking their steps, Missouri went to survey the harvest of delights on the supper table.

Stomach rumbling, she helped herself to the bean-pot, a chicken leg, some heavenly-soft-looking golden biscuits, a scoop of green beans, and some pickled cucumbers, saving room for dessert. Moving next to Susan's chair, she held her plate, ate like a frontierswoman with true appetite, and entertained herself watching the dancers.

Moments later she nearly choked when she saw her baby sister dance by in the arms of Mr. Rye Rawlins.

Missouri was struck with envy. As he turned her sister, she glimpsed wide shoulders, a trim waist and hips, long legs, and that well-formed profile that made her heart beat quickly. He'd left his hat on the hat tree near the door, and his dark hair gleamed in the lamplight. He was smiling down into Faelan's face, deepening Missouri's envy.

Faelan grinned like the besotted youngster she was.

Missouri gapped, and she realized a couple of older women were staring at her. Her cheeks grew warm. Missouri set her plate and fork into a washtub stacked with soiled dishes and made her way to the dessert table.

There, she encountered a tall slender woman with angular features. Her gown was fitted of fine wool in a slate-gray that matched her eyes.

"Hello," said the woman in an East Coast accent, smiling. "I saw you come in with that friend of Mr. Morgan's—Mr. Rawlins, I believe. I'm afraid you've caught me taking a piece of cake for my husband. He's deep in conversation about Mr. Morgan ordering furniture from him."

She held a plate bearing a wedge of raisin cake in one hand and a cake-server in the other. "I'm Mrs. Walker. Darcy Walker."

"A pleasure, Mrs. Walker."

"Darcy does well enough."

Missouri bent her head in acquiescence. "Missouri Harper. Please call me Missouri. So nice to meet someone from the area." It wasn't merely polite conversation; knowing one's neighbors could make a life-or-death difference. "My sisters and I arrived today, you see."

"Oh, I'm afraid I'm a stranger here, too. Been here barely two months. Mr. Walker and I are from closer to Sweetwater Springs, a half-day's ride from that town."

"I'm not familiar with that area."

"If you take the longer route to the Springs, you'll come to our place in the woods. My dearest friend Lina and her husband Jonah Barrett have a farm nearby." She set the server down and turned, gesturing toward a buxom woman with black hair, ringlets cascading about her animated face as she spoke to reserved Mrs. Morgan. "Lina has taken to Mr. Barrett's young son, Adam, as if he were her own. I find that so admirable, don't you?"

"Children steal your heart. I found that with my baby sister when she was born."

Keen to take the only blueberry tart left on a rose-patterned dish, Missouri picked up a plate and set the tart, golden, flaky, and oozing blueberry syrup, onto her plate. Oh, she had waited for this. Manners, she reminded herself, and asked, "Are you acquainted with my aunt, Mrs. William Harper?"

"I'm afraid not. My connection here is through Prudence Morgan. We were—" Darcy set down the plate of cake and chuckled. "Well, frankly, we were mail-order brides from an agency in St. Louis."

Mildly scandalized, Missouri sought to make her new acquaintance feel comfortable. "I recall Mr. Rawlins mentioning that Mrs. Morgan's special guest is from St. Louis."

"Quite right. Miss Bertha Bucholtz was another potential bride with the agency. Prudence—that is, Mrs. Morgan has invited Miss Bucholtz to Morgan's Crossing to run the boarding house. I understand it's in quite a state."

"Our ranch house is in quite a state, too. I foresee a lot of scrubbing going on tomorrow."

Before her new friend could answer, Darcy looked up at someone behind Missouri, her face suffused with feminine pleasure that softened the angular lines.

Missouri chided herself. She was forever looking at the *lines* of people and animals, as she had with Mrs. Morgan, with Mr. Rawlins when he danced with Faelan, with his stallion, earlier today. Well, she forgave herself for that one; she was a horse-breeder and veterinarian, after all. She had learned that good conformation often meant better health, soundness, and longer life. But could she just enjoy the present moment without a judgment? She would try.

Darcy smiled. *Was it her husband?*

Missouri turned.

"Ladies," said Rye Rawlins, offering a slight bow. "Please excuse the interruption." He nodded cordially to Darcy and held out a hand to Missouri. "Miss Harper, would you do me the honor?"

"Well, I—" A blush swept up her throat to her cheeks. Darcy Walker was bound to notice. Setting down her treasured blueberry tart, Missouri gave her new friend a slight nod, murmured, "Darcy," laid her shawl across the back of a bentwood chair, and extended her hand to Mr. Rawlins.

What piercing pleasure to feel the touch of his strong hand. All thoughts of propriety dissolved in a thrum of awareness, and she went into his arms as though born to.

The violin played a waltz, beautiful and sweeping—the flight of an eagle over a sheer cliff, catching updrafts, circling down, around, around, around. Not one misstep between them. Matched perfectly. Breathless and thrilled, she followed his commanding yet gentle lead, moving with him through dips and turns and whirls.

For a while, she could not feel her feet touch down, only the strength of his arms around her, lifting her through the turns. She felt something take hold inside her, something new, wild, primal. Something instinctive—and frightening.

~

WHEN THE WALTZ ENDED, and when she dared, Missouri looked up into Mr. Rawlins' eyes. What she saw there startled her. He had the look of a man caught in the current of a swift stream, rushing to his destiny. Did he see that in her eyes? Because that's what she felt, too.

"Miss Harper," be began.

"Missouri."

"Missouri. I feel—er—" he hesitated, apparently to choose his words. "You are a fine dancer. The best I've known."

"You seem quite experienced, Mr. Rawlins."

"Rye," he clarified. "May I?" Without waiting for an answer, he swung her into a two-step, turning her out and bringing her back against his muscled chest, where she wished she could nestle for the rest of the evening, and into winter, spring...

"Or Ryenald, if you prefer," he added, apparently not apprehending her reverie.

Ryenald, she said in her mind, analyzing the *lines* of it, the soundness. "An unusual name."

"Ryenald Aaron."

Ryenald Aaron Rawlins. A strong name, like him. Substantial and old world, really. "Irish?"

"Scots/English. It's a change from Ronald." He swept her in a dizzying turn, and then the violin ceased.

But only briefly. Another two-step commenced, and he turned her quickly three times in a row.

When Missouri came back into his arms, she was laughing. "Tell me more," she said.

"Only if you'll dance with me for the rest of the night."

"I mustn't. I'll scandalize my family and Mrs. Morgan's guests."

"Mrs. Morgan herself, more like." He grinned to soften the sarcasm. "I suppose I must give you up, then."

But he didn't.

Instead, he swung her into another waltz. They moved in tandem, threading the crowd, dipping and whirling, and she was giddy.

People peered at them, talking behind a raised hand, a fan, a Stetson. *Three dances in a row.* But here in the Wild West, wasn't that acceptable?

Across the room, two men danced with one another, braced apart as if by barrel stays and clomping around with mighty steps.

She'd seen men dancing before, on evenings when the wagon train circled. Someone played the mouth organ and plucked the Jew's harp. The men jostled and romped in the firelight. Sometimes the young women or the husbands and wives frolicked apart from the bachelors. Apparently it was done here, too, in a mining town with a dearth of women. The custom gave the town a certain old-fashioned camaraderie and joviality.

Did that openness mean she could keep dancing with the same gentleman? Her aunt's advice to Jessamine came to her. *You'll get some criticism. But don't pay it any mind. Be true to your nature.* Well, she'd never felt so attuned to her nature as she was in the arms of this Montana stranger. And, she told herself, you will have years ahead, as a spinster rancher, to remember this wonderful night and this last dance. Satisfied she was in the right, Missouri tilted her face to her partner's and said, "You were telling me about your name...?"

"I was named for my uncle, John Aaron Rawlins," he said, his arm strong and steady at her back. "He served under General Grant in The War. Afterward, he was appointed Secretary of War and stayed in Washington."

"And is he serving under Mr. Cleveland?"

Alas, the song ended. Rye escorted her toward her family. "Uncle John died of consumption five months after he was appointed. I'm told Mr. Grant felt the loss."

"I'm sorry, Mr. Rawlins—Rye."

"Thank you." He gave her a slight bow. "I believe you're going to be much in demand for the rest of the evening, Miss Missouri. There's a line waiting just there."

Flushed with the dancing and conversation she'd enjoyed so thoroughly, Missouri gazed in displeasure at the straggle of rough-looking men lined up and watching her, obviously waiting.

Another circle hovered near Susan. Her sister shook her head, refusing a small fellow wearing a bright yellow cravat, patched tweed breeches, and a homespun shirt.

Jess was deep in conversation with Aunt Gwen and the mammoth gentleman Bethesda.

At the far end of the dessert table, Faelan, minx that she was, was regaling Darcy Walker and a slender well-dressed gent with her, apparently Mr. Walker. He held the hand of a boy-child with dark hair and features, meanwhile attending to the chatterbox, an indulgent expression on his face.

"If it's not too much trouble, Rye," she said, turning him aside, "could you escort me to Mrs. Morgan? I want to thank her for the lovely party and ask for a plate of food for Rio."

"Leaving already?"

"I'm afraid we'll all be up at dawn, seeing to the animals, the repairs, the unpacking."

"It's Sunday," he said.

"We'll say our prayers at breakfast. I'm sure the Lord will understand. But we must get settled and make preparations for winter."

"Then I volunteer to assist."

"Oh, we'll manage——"

"I insist," he interrupted. "I have the day off. Mrs. Morgan has persuaded Mr. Morgan to ease up on the men's shifts at the mine on a Sunday, so we get a day off now and then."

With that, obedient to her wish, he brought her to Mrs. Morgan, who was conversing with Mrs. Barrett, the buxom, ringleted friend of Darcy's.

Mrs. Morgan turned an austere look upon them, but her gaze softened when she saw Rye. "Ah, Mr. Rawlins. You've certainly kept our new neighbor occupied tonight." To Missouri she said, "You've quite the talent for a turn about the boards, Miss Harper."

Was it a criticism? Missouri smiled but gave no quarter, inclining her head.

"Ladies." Rye bowed with enough courtliness to melt Mrs. Morgan's icicles. "I'll escort the Harper ladies to the ranch, and then I'll be back to help Mr. Morgan clear out those who have imbibed a bit too much and to help bring the chairs to their respective owners. Miss Harper, here, wanted to bid her adieus."

Missouri swept right in on his rails. "Mrs. Morgan, on behalf of my sisters, I want to extend our thanks for your cordial welcome. It was a wonderful social, and the punch was especially tasty."

Mrs. Morgan drew herself up. "Thank you, Miss Harper. Won't you take some biscuits for the morning? You'll not yet have set up your housekeeping."

"I'd be obliged if I could take some food to our foreman. He's probably faint from hunger by now. We've traveled all day." She cast a look back at the food table. "I'm afraid the biscuits have been eaten, every one. They were so tender and moist. Like eating a cloud."

Prudence Morgan's face virtually glowed from within. "Why, Miss Harper, how nice of you to say. It took many trials to bake a good biscuit." She glanced across the room at her good-looking husband, and something in her softened. "I was told once the missing ingredient in many of my batches was—" now she gazed back at Missouri "—love, Miss Harper. Love is the secret ingredient."

"I'll keep that in mind."

With a mysterious, rather penetrating look at Rye, Mrs. Morgan glanced back at Missouri. "Shall I see you at three tomorrow afternoon, then? Is that convenient?"

"It is." Though it really wasn't. She'd be knee-deep in work.

Mrs. Morgan dipped her head the minutest fraction and turned to converse with Lina Barrett. They'd been royally dismissed.

Rye walked Missouri to Faelan, who objected to leaving and then said reluctant good byes to Darcy and her husband.

Missouri glanced at the dessert table. The blueberry tart was gone, though she hardly cared, she was so happily tired. The three of them moved like a round-up crew to gather food and family including Aunt Gwenllian for the walk home.

And in Missouri's heart, she wondered how she would ever keep from falling in love with Rye Aaron Rawlins of the San Francisco Rawlins.

CHAPTER FOUR

At dawn, dressed in men's clothes, her hair caught in a thick braid down her back, Missouri had been up for a half-hour, lighting lamps and chopping kindling from a cache she found at the far end of the porch. She'd swept off and lit the mammoth iron stove in the kitchen to warm the room, which put out prodigious heat. The coffee steamed in their camping pot, sending off woodsy scents that stirred her appetite...

...if not for the other odors--the familiar scent of smoke mingled with something like rotten cabbage and moldy cardboard.

The rooms of the ranch house had been playground, food source, and sleeping quarters for fur-and-feathered friends. Last night she and the girls had had to clear away scat from one of the rooms so they could lay down their pallets and sleep.

Missouri stepped over torn-off swinging doors and stood inside the opening that led from the dining and huge living area to the giant kitchen. Standing with her fists jammed into her waist, she surveyed the mayhem and felt appalled.

Broken glass.

A rusted tin can gnawed by strong teeth.

A mildewed rag.

The door to the left of the stove had been smashed by a black bear. (She'd plucked hairs from splinters in the frame). She'd forced the door back into shape and braced it up with a chair she'd found in the great room.

Dust covered every inch that was not otherwise claimed by detritus. Stains the origins of which she did not want to guess marked the floors and walls.

A blizzard of flour and cornmeal glazed counters, open drawers, cupboards hanging by one hinge, floors, and a broken chair. The tracks of raccoons, mice, the bear, and even birds wrote the history of the kitchen's visitors. Crumbs winnowed by tiny teeth lay scattered on the floor.

A yellowed almanac, the corners chewed away, lay under the kitchen table. On the wall above the sink, an advertisement from *Lady's Friend Magazine*, picturing the latest fashion for 1870—a full-skirted, pinafore-style gown with layer upon layer of ruffles—hung sideways, stained orange, the cardboard backing warped along one edge.

Seeing Aunt Gwen's dreams in ruins hurt Missouri.

Well, not just Aunt Gwen's but her own and the girls' dreams, too. They'd expected a mansion—*no, don't go over that again. Accept what you find. Be grateful.*

This morning she would try to piece the kitchen back together and make the fixtures and cupboards serviceable, both for Auntie and for the girls and Rio, who would take his meals with them.

Ahora is el momento, she thought in Spanish, taking up the broom Rio had brought from the barn. *It's time*...to attack this mess.

She brushed at counters, the table, and the floor, swept a great deal of the filth into a pile, and using the cardboard advertisement, she collected and dumped the mess into an orange crate.

Setting the broom aside, she dusted her hands and opened a few intact cupboards to see what Auntie had left behind. In one, a cast iron skillet. In a lower cupboard, something gleamed dully. She bent, peered cautiously in. *Metal. Copper.* A copper steam cooker. A blessing! Such an invention saved countless hours of cooking because it steeped the food under pressure. The cooks at her university had used them.

Encouraged, she opened other cupboards, finding a splatterware coffee pot, a stack of heavy stoneware plates, a few four-tined forks, six spoons, heavy mugs, some kitchen cloths, a can opener with a cutting wheel and turning handle, a pot-metal food grinder, and more.

Missouri's spirits lifted. Everything was dusty and needed to be washed. But this was a treasure trove and she was grateful.

On the floorboards above Missouri's head, her sisters were thumping about like muskrats. They would be pounding down the stairs in a few minutes, tomboys that they had become, and she had plenty of chores in mind for them.

Moving to the porcelain-coated cast-iron sink, she faced a setback at seeing the dirt and mouse droppings, but it could have been worse. There could have been dead things. Best of all, a tall metal hand-pump anchored the far end of the four-foot rectangular sink. Would it work?

She pumped the handle a few times to experiment. On the sixth squeaky down stroke, cold water gushed out, sweeping the crusty bits down the drain.

Thank God. I'm saved.

~

As the rising sun spread a syrupy pale glow over the western mountains, Rye stepped up onto the shallow porch, knocked, and stood back. His breath fogged the air.

The door squeaked open. Widow Harper peeked out, smiled when she saw him, and came out of her cabin carrying a pan covered in a frayed red kitchen cloth.

"Biscuits?"

She nodded. "Ready to bake."

He took them and, out of habit, grasped her elbow, helping her down the step. Releasing her, he picked up the satchel of food he was bringing to the Harper ladies and slung the strap over one shoulder.

The thought of soon seeing one particular redhead gave him an abnormal heart rhythm. He wanted to race to Missouri and catch her with her night-braid coming loose around that slender throat.... He indulged in a remembrance of their dances. He would never forget.

Gwen tugged a knitted-and-patched brown shawl around her shoulders. "All set." She held out a hand for the biscuit pan.

He gave it. "Is that enough to keep you warm, Miss Gwen?"

"You make a woman feel young with that nickname, Rye. I reckon I'll be indoors helping my nieces get things in order."

She took his arm, as she often did on their walks, and they moved slowly toward the plank bridge. "If they're anything like their mother, that old stove will already be fired up and warming the place till you can't get your breath."

He laughed.

It was but a ten-minute walk--left after the bridge,

through the trees, into the open, up the incline to the flats. As they came into the yard, he saw lamplight at the barn and knew the foreman, Rio, was feeding the stock. He seemed a good sort. Quiet but decent.

By the time they approached the ranch's porch, Gwen's breath clouded around her face in short pants.

He slid his hand to her wrist. Her pulse was fast. He worried she was unduly stressing her heart.

"Easy now," he said. "Don't want to worry your girls."

"And you're not to say a word about my condition to them," she said, her tone stern. "Promise me."

He hesitated. "They're your kin."

She tugged on his arm, stopping him, and stared. "Ryenald Rawlins. I'll keep your secret if you'll keep mine."

The silver hue in her retinal arteries clouded her blue eyes. He suspected the discoloration was related to her hypertensive heart. Rye wished he had von Ritter's new sphygmomanometer to get a better reading. He'd read about the new device in the medical journals sent to him from a friend at St. Mary's Hospital in Frisco. Those periodicals were his only ties to his old life. He'd left the medical profession and his family behind. *Rightfully so. He did not deserve any of it.*

Gwen tugged on his arm. "Rye...."

"Have you been taking the herbs?" he asked.

"I have, though the garlic is distasteful. Now, promise me."

"I'll promise not to say a word today."

She held his gaze for another moment and must have seen his determination not to make a blanket promise, because she nodded. "Let's go in and see if anyone's hungry."

"Be happy to, Miss Harper. I'd be glad to draw some water for you, too. For the morning coffee."

"That would be kind, Mr. Rawlins. The buckets are at the back of the first wagon, just there." She waved toward them and then brought her hand to her throat. She was touched by his good will. "Thank you."

He made her a shallow bow and headed off, his stud looking round like a loyal and jealous dog as Mr. Rawlins took the ropes from the hitching post and moved off with her horses.

Faelan had been right. Rye Rawlins was her gentleman caller. He'd shown his colors because he'd been unable to stop himself. The feminine part of her felt thrilled; the horse-farmer head-of-household became alarmed.

She had not counted on falling for any man in the next three years while she proved up this land. It would take everything in her to provide for her sisters, and apparently her aunt and the livestock. This didn't even count establishing a veterinarian practice, which was her dream for the distant future.

Love had no place in these plans. Spinsterhood was her lot.

But she could enjoy a dance and a friendship, could she not? If her heart beat faster at the thought, well, she deserved at least that much.

HOLDING their hems out of the dirt—all but Jess, who insisted on wearing clean dungarees and a shirt tucked in —they trooped through the woods to the wooden bridge that had no rails, and went down along the wide dirt street that led between tents and a hodgepodge of cabins.

Mr. Rawlins walked beside her, leading his stud.

"I'm starving," he said, and, at the thought of eating breakfast with Missouri, felt his own heart pick up rhythm.

～

OWING to his height and his commanding presence, Rye took up considerable space in the kitchen. Missouri found it difficult to concentrate upon the task of frying fatback. He was two feet away, bent on one knee, holding a screwdriver, frowning at a hinge. He'd already repaired the swinging doors leading to the dining and great rooms.

She watched him from the corner of her eye. To see him so close gave Missouri strange palpitations. The dark sideburn, the grooved cheek, the strong shoulder, the well-formed hands with trimmed nails.

"Smells good," he said, canting a look at her.

She jerked her gaze away, her cheeks bloomed, and she turned to her task.

Cowboy, the tabby, looked up from his bed, a fox pelt in a low-sided wooden box near the stove, as if to say, *What's all the stir about? Where's my piece of bacon?*

With the café doors repaired, Missouri felt isolated from her Aunt Gwen and the girls, who were chattering as they swept and dusted the reception and dining rooms, oblivious to Missouri's rocketing emotions. Her curiosity about the man beside her, his manliness in such close proximity, brought new feelings and she felt vulnerable.

"Have this done in a jiffy," he said.

"Will you take breakfast with us?"

"I will, thank you. I could eat a basket of briars."

She smiled. "Well, it'll be tastier than that."

"The smell of that bacon is near to making me faint," he said, humor in his tone. "Hong Guan, one the Chinese miners, raises the finest pork I've tasted. We're lucky to have him in Morgan's Crossing."

"It was kind of you to bring us a piece. It smells heavenly."

Faelan burst open the kitchen door—good that Missouri had removed the chair. A basket over her arm, hay stuck in the pompadour of chestnut hair she'd piled rather forward on her head, she announced, "The chickens got shut in the barn last night. I had to hunt through the hay to find the eggs. Ten. They're laying nicely."

"Easy on the door, pet," admonished Missouri, setting Aunt Gwen's biscuits into the oven.

Faelan looked back at the framework as if a stranger had snuck up behind her. "What's wrong with the door?"

"A bear broke through. I've only snapped it back together, but it's wobbly."

"I'll take a look at it," said Rye, twisting a screw into place.

Faelan set the basket of eggs on the counter near the stove. "You're ever so handy, Mr. Rawlins. Want me to help you?"

One last twist of his wrist and he stood up.

His nearness caused an inner shiver in Missouri. She poked furiously at the slices of salted pork sizzling in the pan.

"That should do it," he said, shutting the cupboard, which didn't even squeak. He grinned at Faelan. "You can help me take a look at that door."

The two of them went onto the wrap-around porch, testing the door, getting tools, hammering a board across the outside to strengthen it. In and out, in and out they went, talking about the chickens and the foal and the wild beasts that came to the edges of town sometimes, while

Missouri drained off the fatback slices and fried bread and eggs.

She dug into the sack Rye'd brought for her and found a small bag of dried fruits and berries, a jar of blackberry preserves, and a can of peaches. To this trove she added a crock of butter they'd made three days ago on the trail. She set everything on the table, the varnish gleaming from the scrubbing she'd given it.

Susan peered into the kitchen. "Auntie wants to know if we're eating in the dining room or here in the kitchen."

"Kitchen, don't you think?" Missouri rinsed mugs and set them to drain. "We'll need seven places, but I think we can squeeze in. Where is Mama's blue and red tablecloth? That should do."

"I'll get it." Susan disappeared.

"Faelan, fetch Rio," Missouri said, taking out the biscuits and placing them on a trivet. "Time for breakfast."

"Alright." Faelan fired off at a run. Always at a run, that one.

Rye came indoors. "I don't see a wash basin outside. May I use your sink?"

"I left a tub of warmed water there for you. A bar of soap above the sink. Towel on the edge."

He began to scrub his hands at the sink.

Was this how it would feel to be married? Her husband busying himself with repairs and making companionable talk while she cooked? That ever-present man-energy setting her pulse racing?

Would she ever know the easy friendship of a loving, helpful man who also shared her bed? She couldn't marry for several years—to do so would risk the girls' interest in their land. Yet this man, so kind, so funny, so friendly, and clearly so competent, would soon find himself a wife and no longer fill Missouri's kitchen with his goodness and woodsy scent.

Sad at the thought, she covered the stack of fried pork and platter of eggs with clean cloths and set them on the shelf above the cooktop. *What have I done to myself—this journey, this risk, this terrible burden of family and land?* Though of course she'd thought about marrying someday, until this moment, she hadn't realized what her choices would cost her. Why had she come here rather than begin her practice as a veterinarian in Missouri and eventually settle with a husband and raise a family?

At that moment, Aunt Gwen, Susan, and Jessamine crowded into the kitchen, faces shining with exertion and the joy of feminine company, and she answered herself. *They are my reason, my motive, my goal. Their happiness and safety.*

She turned to them, handing a stack of plates to Jess, a handful of flatware to Susan, some hand cloths to Aunt Gwen, and with Rye and her family bustling and laughing, she once again made peace with her decision.

CHAPTER FIVE

They crowded around the table, Aunt Gwen taking a seat "to get the heat from the stove," and Missouri at the head nearest the kitchen door so she could serve from the stove, when Faelan's boots pounded across the side porch.

"*Missy*," she hollered, her tone hoarse with fear.

Missouri jerked to her feet. "What—?"

Faelan flung open the door and plowed to a stop before Missouri. "Missy! Oh, Missy. He ate something, he's sick—"

"Who?"

"Traveler."

The foal. Last of the Harper stallion's get, that magnificent stud who'd made their horses famous. The stud had died under her father, struck by lightning.

Panic ripped through her. She tried to keep calm. "Go ahead and eat. I'll see to him."

She hurried to the salon, grabbed a shawl and her medical bag from the hat rack near the front door.

Once outside, she crossed the porch, leapt down to the yard, and rushed toward the barn.

Traveler. Can't lose him. Seed to the future. Wonderful lines, friendly disposition. Dear Lord, she prayed, unable to articulate the words. *Dear Lord.*

She ran through the clutch of pecking chickens, scattering them, sending them squawking. She'd been to the barn once this morning to take a mug of coffee to Rio, so she knew the layout. She hurried across the threshold, into the dim interior.

The heads of nine of their equines came over the stall doors to stare at her, some of them with their mouths full of alfalfa. Not one nickered, as a few had this morning. Even the cow in her own stall peeked over, grinding her food.

Tension lay heavily in the old barn.

Which stall? She glanced around, frantic, before realizing the one down the aisle had no animal peeking over.

She hurried to the half-door and swung it open.

The special stall was roomy, meant for a dam and her foal. Straw lay scattered on the floor. Hay lay in a corner, mussed but not eaten. Dancy stood against the back wall, black muzzle lowered to sniff and chuff at the foal's face.

Traveler lay on his side, legs stiff, his breathing labored. There was a pool of runny feces near his tail. A bad sign.

Rio crouched, rubbing the foal's sides. "I think he eat something," said the foreman.

"What?" she demanded. "What did he eat?"

"Maybe some old grain. I don't know. I let him loose in the barn with Dancy last night. I sweep everything first."

"Alright. Let me have a look."

Inspect, palpate, auscultate, inquire. The protocol had been drilled into her brain by her professors.

Taking the stethoscope from her bag, she fitted the aural tips to her ears and bent to the laboring animal. *Breathe*, she told herself, gut tight. *You know what to do.*

Rio went to the colt's head and put his hands on the cheeks. He looked into Traveler's eyes.

"What do you see?" asked Missouri.

"Still white around. Maybe a little getting reddish."

Reddish wasn't good.

"He is in pain," said Rio. "*Pobrecito*—poor little thing."

Abdomen first. She palpated with two fingers, one tapping against the other. The musculature was firm to her touch—too firm. The thumps made a hollow sound. *Trapped gas.*

Now the thorax. She listened. The breathing was fast.

Now heart. It was thundering. She cringed inwardly. Was Traveler strong enough? Did he have the spirit to fight through this crisis? Or was it too late for him?

Traveler rolled his dark upper lip and squealed.

"I know, baby," whispered Missouri. "It hurts."

With the stethoscope, Missouri listened to the thrash of digestive juices and the suck and swish of the working organs. He was gassy.

Without warning the colt kicked, catching Missouri on the left forearm. Pain shot up her arm. *Fool*, she thought. *Colicky horses kick. Be aware.*

She clutched her arm and continued to assess. His undercoat was still glossy, but the outer growth was growing longer with the cool prairie nights, longer than was usual for this time of year. But that was unrelated to what was making him sick. His flanks were damp from stress. One good thing: His muscles were honed from running in the open all summer. *He's strong*, she told herself. *Maybe he can make it.*

Traveler rocked his lower jaw and tried to rise as another cramp raged through him.

Dancy nickered, nudged the foal's head.

He lay back again.

"Is Traveler going to die?" said a tiny voice at the gate.

Missouri pivoted.

Faelan's eyes were swimming.

"I don't know, pet."

"Oh Missy."

Beyond her baby sister were Susan, Jess, Aunt Gwen, and Rye, none of them eating breakfast as she'd ordered, all of them looking worried.

"Warm water," she demanded, not caring who brought it. "Mix a watery bran. Get blankets."

Rio stood up. "I will do it."

"I want his halter," Missouri said.

"I'll get it," said Faelan.

When Rio left, Rye came into the box and knelt by the young horse. "May I?" Without waiting for her answer, he ran his hands over the chest and distended stomach. He put his finger against the artery in the throat and waited. "Quite elevated," he said softly.

"Yes," she said, feeling inordinately grateful to have him near. "Colic."

"Here," said Faelan, handing the head straps to her.

Missouri gave the halter to Rye. "Would you?"

When he'd gently eased the halter onto the colt's head, he said, "You seem to know what to do."

"I'm a veterinarian. But that's no guarantee I can save him. I've had very little experience."

He nodded.

Faelan whimpered and said, "Oh, Missy!"

Being from a horse-farming family, they all knew the risks to the colt's life.

"All right, dear," Missouri heard Aunt Gwen say. "Let's go and keep the food warm for everyone."

"I want to stay," Faelan said, her tone obstinate. "He's my darling."

All the animals were Faelan's darlings. The sweet-natured child loved everyone.

Missouri and Rye got the colt to his feet. He swayed, and they eased him around the enclosure. "Just gentle movements," Missouri instructed. "Everyone be very calm. Keep him calm."

Dancy followed them close behind, almost as if the dam was grateful they were doing something to help her youngster.

"Susan and Jess," said Missouri, walking between the colt and Rye. "Get a rake and take out this straw. Get that tube from the wagon. Heat more water, but just so you can put your elbow in it and not feel the heat."

An hour later, Missouri sent her sisters to the house to eat and prepare plates of food for herself, Rye, and Rio. For the next few hours, Missouri doctored the colt, making sure she got plenty of water down. Working together, Rio, Rye, and Missouri nursed him, walked him periodically, checked his pulse, hydrated him, and took the best care of him they could.

Eventually Rio and Rye excused themselves to do chores.

The day wore on, Faelan visiting Traveler and then shadowing her new hero. As Missouri ministered to Traveler, the youngster reported that Rye had repaired the porch, carried barrels and boxes of provisions, filled buckets of water. In the afternoon, she reported, "Mr. Rawlins is fixing the fencing in the paddock with Rio."

The man's generosity was overwhelming. He seemed to have always been part of Missouri's family, yet she'd only known him two days.

Meanwhile, the colt walked and squealed and nipped at her sides. The family ate, worked, nursed the sick horse, and said their private prayers, and somehow, hours later, night fell. Lanterns hung on the framework above Dancy's stall door, sending meager light into the space.

Tired but hopeful, Missouri led the foal into the stall, where Dancy was finishing her hay

Rye entered the barn and leaned over the half-door, looking handsome despite lines of weariness around his mouth and eyes. "I'll be heading home," he said. "I've got the early shift at the mine tomorrow."

"I can't believe we've kept you here all day," she said, straightening up. Untying the lead to Traveler's halter, she crossed to stand before Rye on the inner side of the door. A squiggle of tension went through her at seeing him near— a strange longing, as if she wanted to lay her own weary head against his chest and listen to the beat of his heart— the same wish she'd felt when he was holding her close for the waltz. *Into winter, clear till spring....*

"I can't thank you enough," she said.

"Oh," he gestured. "I had myself a good time today."

She gave him a wry grin. "I can't imagine how you'd feel about actually having a day off."

"I'd be bored."

"I know. I would, too."

He angled his head toward the colt. "How is he?"

"He might make it. Around midnight or so I should know."

"Want me to stay with you?"

"Thanks, but Rio will be here." She sent an assessing look at the young stud. "I'm beginning to be optimistic. Traveler's got heart. Like his sire."

"Well, Morgan will want me early...."

Morgan. "Oh my!" She gasped. "I forgot about my visit with Prudence Morgan."

Rye laughed. "That's right, you have."

"I've insulted her," said Missouri in dismay.

"I doubt you'll live it down."

She squinted at him. He was teasing. "Well," she said. "If Mrs. Morgan can't forgive me for missing tea while my horse was dying, I guess I don't need her friendship."

Rye smiled, putting crinkle lines around his fine blue eyes. "I wouldn't go that far. She'll understand. Besides, here in this small town, we all need each other."

When he was gone, Missouri absently rubbed Traveler's flank. *Was he giving good advice or courting her?* Either way, she agreed with him. She was beginning to think he was indispensable. How was she going to keep from falling for him?

CHAPTER SIX

Over the next few days, Traveler recovered, to Missouri's unending relief, although they never found the source of his illness. The nights grew colder, and the family established a routine.

One day, after helping Rio and Missouri feed the stock and milk Stowe, Jess organized the bills and journals she found in the desk in the great room to make room for her writing materials. She began to jot notes. No one knew what she was writing. Jess was usually quiet about her creations until they emerged complete.

Missouri had sent Faelan to Prudence Morgan's house with a note of apology for missing her tea invitation. Her youngest sister had probably regaled the woman with the details of saving the sick foal, because Faelan came home with a pocketful of molasses cookies for her trouble. Apparently Mrs. Morgan wasn't holding a grudge.

A few days later, Susan and Jessamine helped Aunt Gwenllian move back to the ranch, where she took over the running of the kitchen and the overseeing of the household tasks.

~

Mr. Rawlins leaned close to be heard above the laughter and talk, the violin music and the *tang* of flatware. He said in Missouri's ear, "I'll check in with Morgan. Tell him and Mrs. Morgan you're here." With that, Mr. Rawlins was gone.

Missouri felt irrationally abandoned. She watched him thread his way to a man with brown hair and wide-set handsome eyes, a man dapper and confident, like Mr. Rawlins. Beside him was one of the most self-possessed women she'd ever seen. Not even Mrs. Grover Cleveland, in her elevated position, touted in the papers, seemed as proud.

In the press of the crowd, Missouri felt shy. Her corset pinched. On the prairie she was used to being free. She and her sisters hadn't been in proper society for months.

At home, the girls had worn mourning gowns. But while planning to move to the West, they'd decided to leave grief and black behind. There would be fewer explanations and less vulnerability to men bent on taking advantage of orphaned young women. Rio, of course, had been ever watchful on the journey. But he eschewed society and would not come with them tonight.

Though several ladies wore styles of the past, her own gown was just last season's, so that gave Missouri a boost. Mrs. Morgan bore herself proudly and wore a silk gown the color of a lake in the late afternoon; it was trimmed in russet grosgrain ribbon and drawn up into a bustle. Very elegant. Her circle of friends dressed in various degrees of fashion, mostly in muted colors, some fine and others plain.

At that moment, Missouri's sisters clustered around her,

Rye, Rio, and the whistling Beth Janes had brought Aunt Gwen's bed, rocking chair, bookcase, and bureau from the cabin and installed them in the main upstairs bedroom, where she could look out at the river and town.

Susan took the room next to Gwen, while Faelan and Jess shared a third bedroom. They'd cobbled together canvas and wood to replace the broken window.

Missouri took the last bedroom on the north end of the house. From the window she could see the mountains and the bunkhouse, garden, and barn, which were now her focus.

Gwen's warmth and loving manner became a fulcrum around which the girls' temperaments and lives revolved. All the girls seemed to enjoy the dawn-to-dusk work of setting the place in order, buoyed by a sense of family they'd missed since their parents passed away in that horrendous fall storm.

Susan and Aunt Gwen typically rose at dawn and set the day in motion with fire, coffee, and simple breakfast fare. Faelan, their runabout, was always sent to fetch Rio.

The foreman had moved into the bunkhouse and spent the first night cold, until he'd hammered the damaged wood stove back into useable condition and took a few chunks of wood from under the porch of the main house.

Freed by her family's happy industry, Missouri retired from running the girls' lives. She went to the barn every morning to assess the condition of the stock and take inventory of supplies. She helped Rio care for the animals, oil tack, and fix broken things.

They moved the cow, horses, and mules into the paddock that Rye and Rio had repaired, where they grazed on withered grasses that would not sustain them long. In an unexpected stroke of luck, though, they had hay in abundance in the loft above the main floor, mostly undamaged. The barn, apparently built before the Harpers established their cattle ranch, had withstood harsh Montana storms without succumbing to nature's forces.

However, their grain stores would not last till summer, the earliest they could expect to bring in a crop. That worried Missouri, because working the horses hard, as they would today, meant the animals needed grain to replenish the drain on their energy. Three-year-old alfalfa wasn't enough.

She made a mental note to ask Rye this evening if the ranchers hereabout grew feed crops to sell. She would need to use some of the family's precious funds to buy oats and barley, or wheat, or corn—whatever was available.

She hoped she'd see Rye tonight. He stopped by every few nights after the supper hour, she suspected so the family wouldn't expend their stores of food on him. He stayed a short while for talk, a game of cards, or a sing-along, and then—too soon to suit Missouri—bade everyone a pleasant good night.

Half of her wished he would quit the quick stop-ins, for she looked forward all day to seeing him and was coming dangerously close to losing her heart to the charm of his company.

Well, she thought now, shouldering into a corduroy coat lined with lamb's wool, enough daydreaming. There was work to be done. She snugged on her felt hat and went into the yard.

The sun was out this morning, but the frost crunching underfoot hadn't melted. Her breath clouded around her face. The mountains to the north ranged along behind the barn, capped by a dusting of snow. Beneath the peaks and red cliffs, the deep green of piney woods made a ruffle along the distant edge of the valley. *Not covered in snow yet. Good.* It was to those woods she was bound today.

As she stepped around the chickens and entered the great dim barn, she heard Rio mucking out a stall about midway down the row.

"*Hola*," she called.

"*Como estas?*"

"Fine, everything's going fine. Wondering if you have time for a ride."

"Si. Que pasó?"

"*Nada*. We need wood. I want to see how far we'll have to go and how many dead trees we can find. We need to stock up for winter."

"*Vámonos*," he said, coming out and setting the rake against the wall between stalls. He brushed his hands on his leather vest and tucked his shirt into ancient dungarees that had deep, sagging cuffs. Beneath his straw hat, his face looked dark in the scant light, and he'd looped a red-checked bandana around his buttoned collarless shirt. He took a warm duster from a peg and put it on. "Let's go."

They caught and saddled her mare and his mustang, and then they outfitted Vesta and Betsy, the Percherons, so they could drag logs, tying up the singletrees, chains, and driving reins and putting lead ropes on the quiet gray giants. Strapping canteens and axes to their saddles, she and Rio chucked their long rifles into scabbards and headed northeast, following the stream-with-no-name, as Rye called it, away from town.

Twenty minutes later, the tributary veered east toward a huge round mountain. They left the water, striking across the valley toward the red cliffs.

This was her homestead adjoining the original ranch, hers and Susan's. She felt mighty good to be traveling over the land, seeing what they'd bought, what she'd have to prove up to keep possession. Right now the valley was covered with stunted grasses, which indicated a droughty spring and summer. Though, with rain or irrigation, this might be prime land for feed crops and grazing. Missouri allowed eagerness to buoy her spirits.

They crossed a shallow trickle, and this late in the year, that meant it was at least a meager source of irrigation or stock water, or perhaps it was a spring. Even better. She imagined her and Rye setting out on a ride to find the source of the creek....

And then she dismissed the thought because something about Rio's demeanor concerned her.

He gazed across the north end of the valley. The grasses were sparse here, like the head of a man who was losing his hair. "*El invierno,*" he said. "The winter, he is coming."

"I can feel it, too."

"Grasses almost killed this summer."

She nodded.

"Beavers build big houses. Big," he gestured. "Birds leave us early. Hard winter coming. Going to be bad."

A chill swept her spine.

They rode in silence, climbing through arroyos, crossing a dry wash, heading for the tree line. What would "*bad*" mean? How bad? She thought of how her horses' winter coats were more robust than usual for this time of year. Did they sense a bad winter coming? Was their body chemistry preparing them?

A half-mile from the woods, it began to blow, and the wind sent icy fingers around her collar. The temperature dropped ten or fifteen degrees, she guessed. Her nose and cheeks grew cold.

"Going to snow soon," she said.

"*Sí.* Snow bad."

How bad? Should she be worried? Today she wore deer-hide gloves with the fur inside, so her hands remained warm, which reminded her to warn the family to get out their winter clothing. She made a mental note to have Rio check the roofs of the house and barn. She would need to order or buy feed, root vegetables, and jars of fruit. Meanwhile, she needed to think about stringing ropes from house to barn. The longer the list became, the more worried she felt. She wasn't ready for winter.

"Fences," commented Rio, distracting her.

They wove among scrubby pines, and she understood he meant they could cut these stubby evergreens for fence posts. The garden needed to be fenced to keep the cloven-hooved creatures out of what was almost certainly going to be Susan's kitchen garden and orchard. A job for spring.

They rode up a steep hill. She noted the location with a landmark she could see through a stand of hardwoods and pines—an enormous red rock split in two, the crevice wide enough to ride through and the back closed at the top, forming a cave. Split Mountain, she named the place, a haven should they ever need it.

They passed a handful of hardwoods that she could harvest in the spring and season-off for next winter's fires. The horses hooves clicked through fallen leaves. They wound up another hill, turned right to follow a dry creek bed, and came into a grove of what Rio called *los pinos ponderosas*. The pines were big, straight giants.

In a handful of minutes, they found one whose greenery had grayed, the wood probably dry enough to burn now. There were others damaged by insects or the drought. Here was her firewood for the foreseeable future. Now to get a couple of trees cut and hauled.

They dismounted and tied off the horses so they could graze on some sparse grasses up the hill and well away from the work. Then they chopped the first tree in tandem, using both axes—Rio a strike, Missouri a strike—until they'd taken a wedge from the trunk.

Soon Missouri's shoulders were hot and achy.

On the backside of the tree, Rio worked alone.

In twenty minutes, there was a creak, a groan, and the monster came crashing down in a clearing.

One of the horses squealed, but they soon grazed again.

Once she and Rio had found and harvested a downed second ponderosa that would be dry enough to burn this winter, Rio got out his frame saw. While he cut each tree in two sections, Missouri chopped off branches to reduce drag.

Rio wrapped chains around one-half of each tree and used Vesta to draw the halves into pairs. He wrapped each pair with chains. Almost done, they cut wedges from the undersides of the front ends of the logs to make a sleigh effect, to pull more easily.

When they were finished, they drove Betsy and Vesta in line, laid down the singletrees, and made sure the drag chains were straight. That done, they mounted up and took the Percherons' lead ropes.

Rio looped Vesta's lead around his saddle horn to get better power and control.

Missouri did the same with Betsy's.

"*Vámonos*," called Rio, nudging the mustang's flanks. The well-trained gelding jumped forward, stretching Vesta's neck and making her take a step.

"Let's go," Missouri shouted, urging her mount and her own dray horse forward. "Hup, Betsy. Hup, hup!"

The docile animals lunged and tugged to get the heavy logs moving. Soon they were out of the woods and headed down into the valley. The wind was at their backs, probably chasing across the snow out of the Bitterroot Mountains.

Missouri had the satisfaction of knowing their home fires would blaze tonight. Four or five more trips like today and they should have enough wood to last into spring. Her shoulders twitched just thinking about the work.

And then she remembered she'd see Rye tonight, and she forgot about the hardship.

～

ON OCTOBER 5, completely unexpectedly, a troupe of entertainers arrived in Morgan's Crossing. Rye was amused by a short bald fellow with a lot of words in his mouth who showed up at the mine and invited the workers to spend a nickel to see the show.

On his way home after work, Rye rode by the crossroads and saw the circled caravans—one painted in garish black with gold trim, a second in green, and another in purple with lavender accents. Colorful banners hung on the sides of the wagons, depicting dancers in low-cut clothing, musicians, and acrobats. The party's horses and dogs had been staked out in pens, and a couple of violinists practiced on chairs set in the withered grass.

A veteran of two mine gangs, Rye had never seen such entertainments in a mining camp, and he immediately thought of Missouri...of giving her some relief from the routine and hard physical labor of ranching.

After feeding Bart, sprucing himself up, and changing into his good clothes, he hurried to the Harper Ranch to invite the women to attend a night of entertainment at the meeting hall at seven o'clock.

When he knocked on their door, Susan admitted him, listened to the news, and served him coffee. Then she left him to wait in the sitting room on a gray overstuffed chair, eager to see Missouri.

Susan sent Faelan running to the barn to get her.

Missouri arrived moments later, scraped mud from her boots, and came inside. She wore baggy men's pants and her work coat. Her cheeks were rosy with exertion, her red hair in disarray. Even disheveled she looked stunning.

Out of breath, she sluffed off the coat and hung the garment on the hat tree. "Vagabond entertainers?" she asked him, smiling.

He took the smile to mean she was happy to see him.

"That's right. You all have been working so hard to run this place I figured I'd escort you out for the evening."

"Sounds wonderful. Give us twenty minutes." She urged the women to their rooms to tidy up and dress for the outing.

Ten minutes late by his pocket watch, the five women came down the stairs in much better order than when they went up. They looked fresh and pretty in the same gowns they'd worn to the town dance.

Rye's eyes feasted on the beautiful, voluptuous woman he'd fallen for twelve days ago. Seeing her in the green dress and shawl, her hair pulled up on the sides with a matching ribbon, he admitted to himself his cardiac rhythm went up at least thirty beats.

Fifteen minutes later, taking their time in consideration of Gwenllian's slower pace, they arrived at the cabins.

"Hellooo," called Rye at the fancy iron gate of the last one.

Beth Janes, his mammoth best friend, who'd taken to Jess, came out of his abode singing in a decent baritone,

"As I was a walking down Paradise Street

A pretty young damsel I chanced for to meet...."

Beth lifted a flame-bright lantern. As soon as he spied Jess, he gave a bow and extended an elbow. "May I offer my arm, miss?"

Jess smiled and took his arm, and Rye, amused, led the party to the hall.

At the doorway, Rye and Beth engaged in a friendly shoulder-pushing match to see who paid the nickels for the ladies.

Rye glanced over his shoulder.

Missouri and her family rolled their eyes at one another.

He and Beth decided *sotto voce* to split the cost. They plunked their nickels into the coin box and went in.

Inside the hall, town folk jammed the benches, and lanterns glowed at the windows. In front, curtains marked the stage area, and from the curtain came the sounds of bumping and scraping and the barking of a dog.

A few miners puffed on cigarettes against one wall, sending the wisps curling toward the ceiling and adding the scent of burnt tobacco to the air.

Michael Morgan hurried to the men. From his annoyed expression and gestures, he wasn't pleased with his miners. After a few words, the fellows clomped outside in their heavy boots.

Hoping to find seats together, Rye's group of seven moved down an outside aisle but the room was already crowded. Gwen, Susan, and Faelan filed in and took seats. With only two spaces remaining, Jess went in followed by Beth, who shrugged and grinned at Rye.

He and Missouri found a place near the back on the aisle. Out of consideration for the people behind them, he removed his hat and placed it on his knee.

The talkative barker who'd come to the mine swaggered onto the stage and welcomed the guests, describing his program in flowery language.

Rye and Missouri looked at each other and chuckled.

He tried to figure a way to ease her hand into his but

realized he'd have to wait for the show to begin, when hopefully only the stage would be lit. He contented himself with the scent of meadows warmed by the sun. Her unique scent always made him want to lean close and kiss her neck.

Truth be known, he was relieved to be distracted when the first act took the stage--a dark-haired juggler. The fellow worked his way up to juggling four balls, and the audience clapped in modest approval.

To Rye's delight, a strawberry blonde in a short flouncy skirt followed the juggler. Whistles and catcalls pierced the applause. Her specialty was acrobatics, and the contortions she went into pleased Rye greatly.

Next came an athletic-looking brunette with two dogs, a miniature poodle and a Jack Russell terrier. The animals wore outlandish hats and net "skirts" matching the woman's outfit. She directed the animals to leap and turn on hind legs. One was made to walk a hoop across the floor and another to jump rope in tandem with his mistress.

Being animal lovers, he and Missouri laughed aloud and clapped.

Each performance ended to raucous applause.

Rye glanced at his companion, then slid his hand to hers and clasped it. She didn't pull away. He read this intimacy to mean she liked him. The hand-holding and the radiance of her smile when she'd greeted him earlier were enough proof to make him fairly abuzz with excitement.

He considered putting an arm around her shoulders, but that wasn't something he'd do in public. He didn't want to make her uncomfortable.

So he turned his attention to the emcee, who introduced a young woman with wavy auburn hair and freckles. She claimed nearly Rye's full attention, for she wore a floor-length sparkly gown that you could almost, but not quite, see through.

Several of the miners stood up, clapping and whistling.

She began to recite poetry.

The men took their seats, listening in apparent rapt attention.

Rye was sorry to see the lissome woman leave the stage, replaced by a comic.

That act came to a close, and two female violinists— the women he'd seen when he rode home from the mine— brought chairs to the stage, sat down, fitted the instruments to their shoulders, and began to play.

Oddly, down front, he saw Beth, Jess, and Gwenllian rise and come up the aisle. People turned to watch them. When they got to Rye, his friends stopped.

Rye took one look at Gwen's face and stood up. "Come," he said to Missouri. "Your aunt's not feeling well."

They moved into darkness and a cool breeze. Jess pulled the lapels of her jacket close and Missouri and Gwen clutched their shawls.

Beth went to the side of the building to retrieve the lamp he'd left in the dirt.

Glancing at his watch by the light of the lamp so others couldn't see, Rye put his hand on Gwen's wrist and counted. Her pulse was one hundred five when it should have been eighty or eighty-five. He needed to get her the tincture to lower her blood pressure.

All the evidence in the world lay open to the viewer's eye in his cabin—the ceiling hung with herbs he'd collected over two summers, the surgical instruments and bottles of medicine, the medical books. If he took the Harpers there, his secret would be exposed.

Faelan and Susan came out of the hall, and now the six

looked at Rye as if he knew what to do. Of course, he did, but that was his secret and Gwen's.

"Does your head hurt, Gwen?" he asked.

"It does, Rye."

He felt her cheek. It was hot. "Feeling faint?"

"A little."

"Is she going to be all right?" asked Faelan.

"What is going on?" asked Missouri, searching Rye's face.

"She's had too much excitement." He turned to the patient he'd treated secretly for two years. "Gwen, remember I taught you to massage that artery in your neck and the nerve that runs beside it?"

She frowned.

Rye placed two fingers against the nerve and gently, gently massaged. His glance took in the others and landed on his best friend.

"Beth, best you carry Miss Gwen. I'm guessing she's feeling a little weak."

"Up you go, Miss Gwen." Beth lifted her with ease and, smiling down at her, asked, "Comfy?"

She nodded.

"Get her home. I'll come by in a few minutes with an herbal tincture that will help her feel better."

"How do you know—?" asked Susan, beginning to walk with the others.

"I have a friend in Northern California," Rye explained. "He's Yurok Indian. I spent a year with him in eighty-four."

"But he's—" started Susan.

"A savage? Yes, by society's standards. But not by mine. He has great wisdom. He's a revered medicine man."

Gwen had heart disease and needed constant treatment, which he'd administered without the knowledge of anyone in their circle. His promise to keep her illness from the girls weighed heavy on his conscience.

"Listen," he said. "Get her home and resting. I'll be there in ten minutes."

Missouri held his arm. "How ill is she?"

"My guess is, enough that she needs to take it easy for a few days. Sometimes her blood pressure spikes. Now, I'll see you a couple of minutes after you get home."

"You're the doctor."

He sent her a quick, shocked look.

Missouri smiled, obviously jesting. She hurried to catch the others, disappearing into the trees at the creek. Their voices faded.

Rye put a hand on his chest, felt the heavy thud of his own heart. Feeling guilty about not telling Missouri about her aunt's condition yet torn to do his duty by Gwen, he went into his cabin to find the bottle he wanted.

A feeling welled up, a deep feeling of discomfort. He realized he was no longer willing to keep Gwen's secret. Her family should know about her medical situation so they could treat her if he couldn't be there. If Gwen refused, he would just have to tell her that if Missouri asked, he would tell her the truth.

He would find a way to talk to Gwen as soon as she was feeling better.

CHAPTER SEVEN

On a Saturday night in the third week of October, Rye rode home from the mine tired and sore. After two years' swinging a pick and hammering up trusses, his body still objected to the punishment.

He unsaddled, unsheathed his rifle, fed and watered Bart, and trudged back into the cabin to gather a change of clothes. A soak at the bathhouse was going to cure what ailed him, but he also had another goal.

He intended to smell good for Miss Missouri later this evening. She was expecting him, but she wasn't expecting what he had in mind. After weeks of friendly visits, he intended to ask her permission to court her.

His conscience tried to warn him that marrying with a secret was a foolish mistake. But he'd hidden his true self so long he half-believed he was a miner with no education and few prospects.

The good side was that he worked like a winter-scared beaver, without pause, and he'd been to the Harper Ranch enough to know he liked ranch life. It was hard but clean and rewarding, better than working like a mole in the dark.

He could help Missouri with his knowledge of medicine. Work beside her to achieve her dream of a successful horse ranch. And he'd seen her speculate about Black Bart's potential as a stud. If he didn't bring truth to the table, at least he brought assets she needed.

What about love? That was the easy part. He'd fallen body and heart for Missouri Harper on the first day he'd met her. He counted himself lucky. He'd never heard of such a thing, but it had happened to him, and he couldn't wait to tell her.

Ask her tonight? Or on Sunday when he was riding with her to meet the other ranchers and see if they had an overstock of grain?

Tonight, he decided. The tension of the decision made his stomach jump. *God in heaven, he was going to propose courtship to Missouri Harper tonight.*

He was crossing the road with his arms full of clothes and his mind full of pretty courtin' words when Big John Thorpe pounded down the road on his red appaloosa stallion. *Trouble at the mine?*

"Doc!" shouted Thorpe, black hair flying. "Doc, you gotta come. "Albert's leg. He's cut bad—"

"Let me get some sponges—uh, cloths and such from my cabin," said Rye, hurrying away. "Leave me your horse."

The big man dismounted and trotted the stud to the gate at Rye's cabin. He tied the beast and raced toward the mine.

Sparing a thought for his ruined romantic plans, Rye dashed into the cabin, flung his clothes down, and grabbed supplies: surgical pads, towels, some rope, a jar of vinegar, a pot of honey, the herbs he'd need, and his suturing materials.

He hadn't needed to suture anyone since coming to

Morgan's Crossing, so the men who watched him patch Albert might suspect his training, but that couldn't be helped. He wouldn't let the man bleed to death to keep a secret.

Besides, as long as Michael Morgan wasn't there tonight, he might slide by with no explanations.

However, if asked, he would simply run out the tired line that he'd watched his uncle, a surgeon, many a time. The irony was, his time with his uncle was true. Dr. Aedan Rawlins had been his mentor and role model. It hurt to know he'd broken the old man's heart.

Shunting aside the memories, Rye chucked everything into a leather bag and went outside.

He couldn't deny a thrill at being called to provide real medical care. The longing to do so never left him, and that was another irony. Hiding his identity as a physician was his cross to bear, and he bore the burden waiting for the next broken finger, the next sour stomach that needed his know-how. The men called him "doc," a nickname for tending their simple ills. But they didn't know the truth about him.

It was dark and the whites of the horse's eyes showed. The animal shied from him and wouldn't let him mount. Cursing to himself, Rye made his heart rate slow down, his breathing even out. "Steady," he said, approaching again.

The animal snorted and quivered but stood for the mounting. Securing his bag of medicinals behind the saddle, Rye dug in his heels, and the horse bolted toward the mine.

A few people were out, and heads turned to watch him ride hell-bent-for leather out of town. There would be gossip, unwanted attention. Couldn't be helped. Albert was hurt and needed him.

Before Rye made the turn around the mountain, he

passed Big John churning along the road. Rye kept going, the red horse huffing now, working to keep the pace. He squeezed with his thighs, urging the animal on.

Ahead he could see the outlying camp with the waterway running by—the maw of the mine, the outlines of corral, lean-to, assay-and-telegraph office with its electric light over the porch. He didn't hear the pounding of the stamp mill. Perhaps the injury had happened there.

Mine workers formed a knuckle of onlookers below the shallow porch of the office, haloed with yellow light.

Rye rode hard to the edge of the gang, threw the reins down, and leaped from the saddle.

"Put the horse up," he ordered. "Don't founder him. He's hot."

"Doc's here, give him room," someone said.

The men parted.

Rye strode through them. "What happened?"

"They were changing the cam and the stamp came down on him," said Tim, a scrawny fellow who wore a yellow cravat to every social event.

On the porch lay the miner Albert Whitney, his brown hair matted with sweat. A bushy beard couldn't hide his paleness.

The fiddler Obadiah was bent over Albert's legs, holding a blanket sopping with blood.

"Doc," said Obie, looking up, his face contorted with worry. "He's passed out. Lost too much blood, I think."

"Let me see."

The pant leg was folded back. The wound ran several inches across Albert's right calf, still seeping blood. But not *pumping* blood, so no artery had been ripped open. A serious wound, nonetheless. The muscle was beginning to swell and turn.

"You did fine, Obie," Rye soothed. "Can you boys get

some lanterns and string them up? Somebody get me a canteen of water, too. And better get a wagon so we can take him home."

Albert came-to. With a growl he tried to sit up.

"Not so fast," said Obie, holding him down. "You're hurt. Doc's workin' on ya."

The man settled. "Cold," he said.

He might be going into shock, which wouldn't help things. "Get him a blanket," said Rye. "Here, Albert, this will ease the pain." He took a folded leaf from the pocket of his shirt, opened it, and tipped a white ball of sap from the *lactuca serriola* plant into Albert's mouth. "Swallow it."

The man grumbled and swallowed.

Someone laid a blanket over Albert's chest.

Rye set his bag of medical tools on the porch step in handy reach, unstopped the bottle of vinegar, and began to wash the wound.

Albert thrashed, but Obie and Tim held him steady.

"Going to stitch you up," he told the patient. The painkiller would take effect soon, and he could begin. "Using a blanket stitch a squaw taught me in California."

"Hear that, Ben?" asked Obie, holding Albert's shoulder. "Doc's going to give you a fancy leg. You'll be so pretty 'ol Tim, here, 'll give you turn around the dance floor."

Albert groaned.

As he set out his simple tools, Rye was uncomfortably aware that Michael Morgan had arrived and watched him from the back of the crowd.

TODAY, Missouri and Rio had made their fourth foray for wood, and she should have been glowing with tired satisfaction. Instead, sitting with the women of her family for their evening visit, she was far too aware of the empty seat, and she detested the reason. Rye had not come by this evening. Weeks of steady visits had worked its magic—or harm—on her heart. She was starting to think life would be miserable without him.

"…the matter, Missouri?"

She glanced up. "What, Auntie?"

"Are you plumb worn out?"

"I am."

"She's plumb something else." Faelan grinned evilly.

Missouri nudged her with a foot and glared.

The window over the sink was dark, and the women, seated around the table in the toasty-warm kitchen, clasped mugs of heated milk. Rye would never visit this late, so they'd changed into nightgowns of white and flow-ered blue and pink, with long johns beneath the flannel and lace. All eyes focused on Missouri.

"Missouri's plumb what?" asked Susan, ever interested in romantic notions.

Faelan picked up her tabby cat under the front legs and put her nose against the cat's. "We know, don't we, Cowboy?"

Cowboy mewed in protest.

Faelan tucked him onto her lap.

"What do we know?" asked Susan, looking from Faelan to Missouri to Aunt Gwen.

"You know," said Faelan, enjoying her secret. "Mr. Rawlins. She's plumb crazy for him."

"Faelan Harper!" Missouri pinched her.

"Ow! It's true. I can see, I can see, I can see with my own two eyes. She's sweet on him. And he's sweet on her."

Missouri's cheeks heated coal-hot. "He's not sweet on me. He's being neighborly."

"Fie, Missy," Faelan taunted. "You like him, say you do."

Missouri turned in supplication to her aunt. "Auntie, make her stop."

Aunt Gwen looked long at Missouri with those silver-blue eyes, clearly trying to see her secrets. Turning to Faelan, she said, "Child, stop your teasing."

Faelan pouted. "Well...." She petted Cowboy, then glanced up through her eyelashes, the coquette. "I can read their faces."

"Aunt Gwen," said Jessamine, setting down a piece of lace she'd been repairing. "Tell us about Uncle William. Did he love the cows ever so much? Did he miss them when he went to the mine?"

"Yes, dear. He missed them awfully. But we didn't have grass enough for the cattle he'd bought, you see. They over-grazed the land. They began to die, and he had to shoot some of them to keep them from starving. Killing them broke his heart. Once he was injured, why, we gave up ranching and went to mining. That was almost three years ago."

Pain worked its way into the creases of Gwen's face, the lines deepened, and her eyes darkened.

"Don't," Missouri said. "If the telling will hurt you."

"No, you'd best know what happened, girls." Aunt Gwen sent that silvery gaze around the table. "What you're trying to do here—especially you, Missouri, because you're out there with the animals day and night—is dangerous. Life here in the West, out on the range, can take your life or change it forever in one wrong move, one misstep, one blink or blunder."

She stopped. Everyone waited.

"Your Uncle William." She sighed as if in longing. "Oh, he had the Harper looks, girls. Red hair, blue-blue eyes, that winsome smile that made a body do his bidding." She glanced at the night-cold darkness. "Goodness, I loved him."

"A blessing that you did," said Susan, laying a hand on Gwen's thin arm.

Aunt Gwen patted Susan's hand. "If I'd loved him more, Susan, I would have had the courage to tell him he was doing wrong. We lost everything trying to make a go of this ranch. He insisted on fine things for me and the best of everything for the ranch, and with what little land there was with this place, we simply couldn't make it back." She bit her lip, looked at the café doors as if her husband was coming through them for a cup of coffee or a kiss.

Missouri shivered. To lose a man you loved so much was too terrible to contemplate. To as good as lose the ranch you'd staked everything on would break your heart.

"I've always been grateful Mama died with Papa," she said, her voice feeble with emotion. "Neither of them could bear losing the other."

"You live beyond the grief," said Gwen. "But you wonder how the days and months go by, and you're still breathing without them."

Faelan's eyes welled. She set down her cup of milk. "Oh, Auntie, don't hurt so. And I can't stand to see you sad." She scraped to her feet, the cat falling away. "I couldn't stand losing *any* of you."

Susan rose and went to Faelan, taking her in her arms. "There, there, pet. Nothing's going to happen to us."

Faelan hugged Susan and sniffled. "But what if we don't have enough land to raise the horses? I can't see Traveler starving or—or get shot."

Susan smoothed Faelan's hair, which was rippling with chestnut beauty in the soft lamp glow.

Jess pushed away her sewing. "We've more than four

times the land Uncle William got when he bought this ranch," she said. "We'll have a much better chance. Won't we, Missy?"

"Yes, of course." But inside she shivered and hoped it was true. "We only need a small herd to begin with. That'll give us time to see what the land can support. And when Jess is twenty-one, we'll buy another homestead to the east of our acres and give the horses more room." That was her plan and a huge risk. Could they do it?

"Now, child," said Aunt Gwen, her tone firm, "sit down here, and I'll tell you what happened to us."

They sipped their hot libations and listened.

Aunt Gwen took a small breath. "Seven years ago September, when William was in the cattle pen, sorting the steers to be sold, one of the animals stepped on his foot. He went down with a shout."

Faelan gasped.

"The steers spooked, milling around and trying to get out of the pen. One of them trampled William, breaking something inside his chest. Since then, William couldn't stand up straight, and it was agony to lie down at night. He could no longer lift a pitchfork of hay or shove a heifer out of the way or mount a horse."

The sternum, thought Missouri. He broke the breast-bone and there was no medical help available. *A tragedy.*

"With the cattle dying--"Aunt Gwen pushed away her cup "--and your uncle unable to run the ranch, all he could do was ask Mr. Morgan for a job as watchman. Will could still tote a rifle. He knew Mr. Morgan gave him the position out of pity." She shook her head. "Walking around in the cold of winter at night was a misery, but your uncle stuck to for two years."

"Why didn't you ever write to us about this?" asked Missouri. "Maybe Papa could have helped."

"William's pride, dear. He said, 'Let them believe we're successful. If they never find out what happened, it won't hurt Michael.'"

"Papa," said Susan softly.

"Will adored his baby brother. Knew he looked up to Will. So I—" Gwen's mouth trembled "—I lied to you. I'm sorry. I prayed many a night for forgiveness and now I beg you all. Forgive me?"

Missouri reached out and took her thin hand, squeezing it gently.

Susan rose and went to hug Aunt Gwen. She murmured, "Oh, Auntie, no need. You were trying to protect us."

Jessamine said, "It'll be alright. We're all here to help you now."

"Thank you, girls. But I feel I need to tell you how things ended for your uncle."

Susan, giving a last hug, resumed her seat.

"If you want to, Auntie," said Missouri.

"Well, he disappeared one fall night. A good part of last winter, men rode into the hills and looked for him."

"Did they find him?" Faelan picked up Cowboy and put her nose into the striped fur.

"No, dear, not till last spring. They found his body at the bottom of a steep ravine about a mile from camp. We never knew why he wandered that way." She looked at her hands, clasped in front of her on the table. "Rye says he didn't suffer."

"Oh, thank the Lord," said Susan.

Killed in the fall, Missouri realized. Both brothers died the same autumn.

Uncle William probably broke his neck. Or Rye was saving her aunt's feelings and not telling her what really happened. She envisioned coyotes, wolves, bear. She'd rather accept Rye's story. Uncle Will had died instantly.

"What is the moral of my tale?" asked Aunt Gwen, gazing into the face of each niece.

"Be careful," piped Faelan.

"You are correct, Faelan. Be vigilant around the live-stock. Always be with someone you trust. You mustn't live in fear, but you must be prepared for the worst in order to survive. You must pray for your safety and the safety of your family." She hesitated. "And you must trust your family to love you no matter what awful truth you have to reveal."

Missouri didn't look at Susan, whose secret lay like lead at the bottom of the sisters' thoughts. Instead, needing to change the subject, she said with cheerful finality, "Now, my dears. Let us sing a song of gratitude. For what a blessing we are to one another."

The women smiled, putting tension at bay. Missouri guessed they saw each other with new and trusting, trea-suring eyes.

As their voices lifted on the old, old hymn, "Awake, Sweet Gratitude, and Sing," Missouri thought of Rye. Had something happened at the mine? Was he all right?

Come back to me. Come back to me.

IN THE MORNING, Missouri sat at the roll-top desk, going over the expenses of their trip West and sorting out what she could afford for grain should she find it locally.

Footsteps sounded on the porch. Someone knocked.

Her heart gave a leap. In case it was Rye arriving early for their visit to the ranches this afternoon, Missouri tucked a loose wave into her chignon, smoothed her shirtwaist into her brown corduroy riding skirt, and hurried to answer.

Through the glass she could see Prudence Morgan gazing toward the bunkhouse, probably noting how sad the paint-less buildings, the garden, the well house looked.

Disappointed, still worried about Rye, Missouri put on a pleasant face, swung open the heavy door, and smiled. "Mrs. Morgan. This is a surprise. Won't you step in and warm yourself? The wind is bitter this morning."

Prudence swept in and looked about. Her expression said, Not *too* bad for a rundown old place.

The girls had scrubbed the floorboards spotless, oiled the tufted maroon leather settee and contrasting gray chairs that formed a cozy ensemble before the stone hearth. A welcoming fire crackled, warming the cavernous room. They'd polished the scattered ornate tables and chairs. These, and the carved oaken desk, gray walls, dark-oak moldings around the ceiling and tall windows, and the three frontier prints on the walls, seemed to Missouri to bespeak their hard labor rather well.

Did Prudence Morgan agree?

The woman was frowning, so it was safe to guess she did not.

Mrs. Morgan removed a wool shawl and matching felt hat accented with a spray of bluebird feathers and handed them to Missouri. "You haven't called upon me," she said, her tone imperious, although she could well have been disguising hurt feelings. "Mohammed must come to the mountain, then."

"I'm so sorry, Mrs. Morgan. I thought Faelan explained…the foal…."

"Of course she did. Talked a blue streak about it. Clever girl, your youngest sister."

Missouri softened. "Thank you. Can I pour you a coffee? A glass of fresh milk?"

"I'm on my way to the mercantile so I mustn't tarry. I came about another matter."

"Is someone ill? Something amiss?"

"No. Although Mr. Rawlins certainly caused a stir going to the rescue of one of the miners last night."

"Rescue, you say?" Missouri could hardly contain her curiosity. "Is the miner all right?"

"Apparently. However—" Mrs. Morgan pressed her lips as if to underscore what she was about to say "—I must beg your indulgence in a matter that will benefit the town."

Missouri stood holding the hat and shawl, feeling unsettled. "You certainly have my attention, Mrs. Morgan."

"Mmm. Well. I want your Faelan to come to me."

For what reason? Missouri couldn't keep the edge from her voice. "Come to you—? In what way?"

The blue eyes captured Missouri's with quiet command. "She's needed, Miss Harper. I teach lessons to the young children four mornings a week. They can become quite...*rambunctious*. I've little experience with children. Your Miss Faelan seems both exuberant and intelligent but also well-mannered." She glanced away, and Missouri had the impression she was reluctant to explain. Finally she said, "They will *like* her, Miss Harper. I wish for her to assist me in their lessons and take in hand any who misbehave."

Missouri felt a pang of sympathy for this plain woman with a will of iron. Perhaps she'd had not sisters. Missouri's life would have been lonely without hers. Besides, Mrs. Morgan's pride must have made asking for Faelan difficult.

"Faelan loves everyone and everything," she said softly.

"Her spirit is open to the world. She would be very well suited to such a task."

"She'll come, then?"

"Well—"

"Don't think I won't give something in return."

"No, I—"

"I've a good education myself. I will instruct her in Latin, comportment, writing—"

"I believe our sister Jessamine will instruct her in that category—writing. She has a degree in English."

"A degree?" One eyebrow rose.

"Three of us have degrees."

"I see. But you're busy with the ranch. The child's education should not be neglected."

"No, you're right."

"Mathematics and geography are essential. I'll see that she gains mastery of those subjects. Are we agreed?"

"She must do her chores first thing."

"I'll need her at eight-fifteen sharp. The children arrive at eight-thirty, and we'll want to be ready."

"Well, you have my approval. But I must ask Faelan if she's willing."

"You mean she won't obey?"

"I don't mean that at all. Out of respect for her wishes, I will ask if she agrees. Either way, she will visit you this afternoon with her answer."

Mrs. Morgan's lips pinched together in disapproval. Then, apparently realizing there was to be no better result, she reached for her hat, set it on her head at a becoming angle, and wrapped herself in her shawl. "I'll wish you good day, then, Miss Harper."

"Good day, Mrs. Morgan. We would be pleased to see you come for tea or coffee any time."

"Hmmp." She sailed out the door.

Closing the door, Missouri resolved: *Don't ever let her bully Faelan.* The woman was capable of it, despite seeming fair-minded and of apparent good moral character. Faelan, that loving soul, would give Prudence Morgan all the love and attention the woman probably craved. And in return, Faelan would continue the education their mother had given her youngest until her death.

Missouri returned to the desk to continue her figures when Faelan appeared in her work britches, straw sticking out of her hair. "Who was that?"

"Mrs. Morgan. She wanted to know if you'd like be her assistant, teaching the children of the miners."

"*Teaching?* What did you tell her?"

"That you must do your chores here first."

"*Chores first?* Oh, Missy! You'll allow me to go?"

"Yes, pet. If you want to."

Faelan spun in circles, crying, "Thank you, Missy. Thank you, thank you!" She pivoted, climbed the stairs, and called out, "Auntie, I'm going to be a *teacher*."

Well pleased and anticipating Rye's arrival, now that Mrs. Morgan had explained why he hadn't visited last night, Missouri chuckled and went back to her figures.

CHAPTER EIGHT

A man's tread sounded on the porch, and Missouri leaped up, smoothing her riding skirt and hurrying to see if the caller was Rye. At the knock, she swung open the door.

Rye smiled. His winter Stetson was cocked up, white shirt and string tie giving a formality to their errand. A flap on his heavy duster billowed in a gust. His horse stood at the rail, angling his head to catch the drift from the paddock.

"Well, Dr. Rawlins," Missouri said, feeling giddy and letting her pleasure show. "How is your patient?"

Rye's face paled. His mouth firmed.

How odd. Taken aback, she stared at him, watching the muscles of his face work. Had Prudence been wrong? Had the man died?

He stepped inside out of the chill, took off his hat, rubbed his hair, and at last a pleasant expression surfaced. "Albert was quite well this morning, I'm glad to report."

"I'm so pleased for you both. Mrs. Morgan said you saved his life. What was the matter with him?"

"Albert cut his leg in the stamp mill." He said it dismissively.

Being humble, she thought.

"I picked up a number of medical tricks from my uncle."

"John Aaron?"

"No, Dr. Aedan Rawlins of San Francisco."

"Ah. How wonderful to have that expertise to help others when there's no doctor here in Morgan's Crossing."

His gaze slanted away, but only for an instant. "You would be able to help out, being a veterinarian."

"Oh, goodness, no, Rye. I haven't had much practice since my internship. And large systems are so different. I wouldn't venture to diagnose and treat humans."

"Well, Missouri, now that we've resolved all the medical issues…does a ride to the Circle K suit you at this hour?"

"Indeed it does, Rye. I'm looking forward to meeting a fellow rancher."

She put on her heavy work coat, gloves, scarf, and hat, and they set out for the paddock and barn to catch and saddle her mare.

Ten minutes later, despite the chilly weather, riding along the river road with Rye was more pleasant than she'd imagined. They talked of his job at the mine, of his wish to leave such work because he didn't like the darkness below ground. She told him about the wood she and Rio had gotten in and of Faelan's new post as assistant schoolmistress to the children of Morgan's Crossing.

Rye chuckled. "She's a wonder. I'm not surprised she's already charmed her way to a job."

They rode a few moments in companionable silence.

Missouri's dun, Cricket, a ten-year-old, was as sure-footed as a mule, and she picked her way around a jutting rock.

As Rye's stallion moved alongside Cricket, the animal crowded the mare, arching his graceful neck and easing his head over her withers.

The mare squealed a warning. Rye pulled the stud away. "Is she in season?"

"I don't think so. The nights are so cold I believe her estrus is reduced or gone."

Missouri took a good long look at the gorgeous lines of the stud, wishing they were riding along together in summer rather than at the advent of winter. "I wouldn't want her bred now."

"Why is that?"

"Too much danger of her foaling in a cold fall and the foal having to survive a bitter winter. It's just too hard on them."

"Huh. I wouldn't have thought of that." He corrected Black Bart again and then sent her an appraising glance. "You're quite a woman, Missouri. I admire your pluck. You've got a good education. You're ambitious. You have fine qualities."

She glanced into his eyes and was disconcerted to feel a tingle of feminine reaction. "Thank you."

"I have been thinking of speaking with you on a certain matter."

She blushed and now could not meet his gaze. Her breath caught. What could he mean?

Cricket took a careful look at the plank bridge across the creek-with-no-name and kept on.

They emerged from the trees and splashed across the wide shallow place in the main waterway. This was the crossing she'd taken weeks ago when she and her sisters had arrived. How much had changed since then.

She'd spent time in the company of this handsome miner, witnessing his goodness, his warmth toward her family, and his concern for Traveler and the other livestock. Missouri often wished she could flirt outrageously and encourage him to court her. But that would not be appropriate given her responsibilities at the ranch.

They turned right, following the southeast bank of what she'd learned was called Morgan's River as it edged the town.

"Missouri?"

Her heart fluttered. "Yes, Rye?"

He pushed Bart ahead and took her reins just under the bridle. He tugged Cricket to a standstill, let go of the reins, and reached out.

Reluctantly she took his hand, and her stomach tightened.

"I like your name."

"Thank you. I like yours, too."

"I've been dying to ask why you're called Missouri."

"Oh," she said, relieved at the mild topic. "When my parents moved from New York to Missouri and started the farm, my father fell in love with the country. When I came along, it seemed fitting to name me after the place where they honeymooned and began a life together."

She tried to pull away, but he held on. "Please look at me."

And she did. In fact, she couldn't look away. She sank into his gaze as a kitten sinks into a woolen nest, completely given over to the safety and pleasure.

"I would take it most kindly, Miss Missouri Harper, if you would allow me to court you."

A tornado could not have caught her more off-guard. Her cheeks flamed.

"Have I startled you, Missouri?"

"Yes, you've quite taken my breath. It's—"

"Don't say it's unseemly, for I have waited these many weeks. I've visited often and come to care for you. My attraction deepens by the day."

Her emotions swirled. *Court her?* No, as much as she longed to say yes, it wasn't plausible given her responsibilities.

"Missouri?"

At last she murmured, "Let us, that is, I care for you as well." She made herself look into his eyes. "But as a friend, Rye."

His eyes darkened. His mouth firmed. "I see. A friend."

"Yes I…will you let us be friends? It would mean the world to me if we could."

He let her hand go. She had hurt him.

"Let me explain," she said gently. "My family is involved in a joint venture. If I marry before my acres are proved up the property becomes my husband's. That would cut out Jess and Faelan. Susan has her own acres, but those will eventually be joined to mine and, if Aunt Gwen wishes, to the original Harper Ranch. When Jess is twenty-one, she'll add to the homestead." She sighed. "This is the agreement between us. Each has pledged to make a go of the ranch and our homesteads. So you see, courting is impossible. I'm—I'm sorry, Rye."

"Not more than I."

She was filled with regret to lose the esteem and attention of such a generous, caring man, and on top of that to cause him pain. In another time, another place…*Yes, Rye, yes, you may court me.*

Rye gave a tug to his hat brim and sat straighter in the saddle. "We'll lose the light if we don't get a move on."

Feeling sad, Missouri lifted her reins, and Cricket started forward.

MISSOURI WAS tense from her talk with Rio and from the uncertainty about the grain. She made a mighty attempt to throw off her dour mood and enjoy the ride to the Circle K.

She supposed Rye did, too, because he began to point out the highlights of the area. They went along the trail until they came to the road to Sweetwater Springs, just at a railed bridge, and took a left. Rye gestured to a roomy spread on their right. "The S Bar D Ranch. They've been here since eighty-two."

After several minutes on the gravel road, far in the distance to her left, she saw a group of buildings—a small wood-frame house and the framework of added-on new construction, a bunkhouse, a large barn, and corrals and enclosures for the animals. Cattle dotted the distant meadows.

In a short while, she and Rye dismounted in front of the house.

A lanky sixteen-year-old emerged from a small outbuilding, smoke pouring from its roof. He ran his fingers through unruly blond hair and smiled shyly. "Howdy," he said, coming up. "'Bout got that elk smoked."

"Bound to be handy come winter," said Rye. "Your boss here-abouts? We'd like a chat if he's not too busy."

The boy ducked politely and went to the door. He knocked.

The inner door swung wide. A tall man peered through the screen and then opened it. He carried a saddle on one shoulder.

"Oh, visitors," he said pleasantly, crossing the porch and stepping down. He laid the saddle over the railing.

When he stepped into the light, Missouri could see he

was an attractive man in his late twenties. His eyes were a vivid blue. He wore a deep-gray western hat, dark hair peeking out where the brim and the crown met, and a gray-plaid shirt tucked into well-worn, trim-fitting dungarees.

He glanced at the boy. "Thank you, Ben. Put that smoked meat into a clean bucket and set it on the porch. We'll can it up later."

"Yes, sir." Ben hurried back to the smokehouse.

"Welcome," said the rancher. He nodded at Rye. "Rawlins," he said, friendly, but not in a tone that said they were intimates.

"'Afternoon," said Rye. "I've brought a newcomer. She has business with you."

Mr. Kincaid's gaze came to rest on Missouri, and there was appreciation there. He tipped his brim. "Ma'am."

"Hello, Mr. Kincaid. I'm Missouri Harper."

"The Harper Ranch across from town?"

"That's right."

"Heard you were homesteading a few more acres."

"That is my aim, God willing."

"Horses or cattle?"

"Horses."

"Well, that's fine. Wish you luck."

"Thank you. I believe we'll need it."

"Won't you folks come into the house for some coffee?"

"I won't keep you, Mr. Kincaid," said Missouri.

"Well, walk with me, then, while I put this saddle in the barn. You can tell me your business."

He hefted the saddle and started across the yard.

She and Rye kept their horses with them and walked with Mr. Kincaid toward the huge barn.

"You see," said Missouri, "we have hay aplenty in the loft, but I fear we'll run short of grain before the spring thaw, and if it's a bad winter, which my foreman says it's bound to be, we'll run out and the horses will suffer."

"You want grain?"

"That's right. If you can part with any."

"I've got some oats I can let go, just to be neighborly."

"That would be wonderful, sir."

"Don't 'sir' me, Miss Harper, if you please. Preston's the name."

"Then it's Missouri."

"And Rye," said Rye, walking beside her.

"I can let you have one hundred fifty pounds," he said.

Missouri's shoulders relaxed. "That will surely get us through."

"Glad to do it, then." He turned and stopped her in her tracks with that startling gaze. "I was pleased to get near to thirty-five bushels the acre, despite the drought."

After negotiations, she paid him his price and tucked away her money pouch, saying she would send Rio to collect the grain.

With the tension eased, Missouri smiled. "Thank you, Preston. I'm beholden. If ever I can do anything for you or yours, please call upon me."

He touched his brim. "Ma'am."

As he disappeared into the barn, she glanced at Rye.

He nodded approvingly, and for some reason, she felt proud he had witnessed her exchange with Preston Kincaid. Surely it helped him understand why she couldn't accept his suit.

"Well done, Missouri," Rye didn't smile, and that told her he was still suffering from her rejection.

∾

FOUR DAYS LATER, on the evening of October 27, when the wind howled around the eaves, Rye knocked on the front door.

Faelan brought him into the kitchen with the fresh scent of the wind and the river.

"Here is our friend," she said, smiling up at Rye.

He held his hat in his hand.

"Coffee, Rye?" asked Missouri, feeling that flutter in her chest that always arrived with him. "Or warm milk?"

"Neither, thanks," he said without looking at her.

Her heart went to the bottom. He would not accept her request to be friends, then.

"I'm here about the weather," he said, settling his gaze on Aunt Gwen. After a pause, he glanced at Missouri. "You mentioned last week you wanted to put up ropes from building to building."

"Yes, before the snow."

"It's coming. If you really want to get this done, I can assist you with that chore tomorrow. I'm off work."

An olive branch? "Yes—yes, that would be so kind of you, Rye."

"I'll help," piped Faelan.

"You have school," said Missouri to her sister while keeping hold of Rye's gaze and trying to discern whether she was forgiven for rejecting his suit.

"Fine. Till tomorrow, then." He put on his hat, snugging it down so low she couldn't see his eyes.

No, apparently she wasn't forgiven. He was only fulfilling some kind of obligation, perhaps to Aunt Gwen.

Disappointed, she remained in the kitchen while Faelan went gaily to the parlor, where she let Rye out into the cold night.

~

A WHILE LATER, someone knocked on the kitchen door. Had to be Rio. Missouri let him in with a gust of frigid air. "Coffee?" she asked.

"*No, gracias.*" His hat, too, was in his hands. If she weren't so sad, she'd appreciate the politeness of the men in her life.

"What is it, Rio? Not the foal?"

"No, Miss Missouri. He is well. But we need to go hunting before the snow. He is coming."

"*It* is coming, Rio," said the fourteen-year-old teacher. "Snow is an *it.*"

"*Si.* The snow, it is coming very soon. We do not have time. Tomorrow I go hunting."

This time, Faelan said nothing. She drank her milk and looked at him over the rim of the mug.

Missouri could see a grin peeking around the porcelain. She shook her head. "Tomorrow I'll be putting up ropes and seeing what else needs to be done to prepare us for winter."

A niggle of doubt plagued her. She didn't want to give up seeing Rye because she hoped working together would repair their friendship. And the ropes were a priority, especially if the snow was coming. Given the icy wind blowing tonight, winter was breathing hard and preparing to roar.

The silence deepened. Missouri was supposed to say, *I'll go with you, Rio. We'll leave at first light.* Instead she said, "We'll go day after tomorrow. First light."

"*No.*" He ducked. "*Perdóname,* Señorita Missouri. Two days is too late. I am going in the morning. There is a valley beyond the red cliff. I think a moose live there."

"Moose *lives,*" began Faelan.

"Shhh," said Susan.

Missouri would never argue with Rio's wisdom. She nodded. "Very well. When shall we expect you back?"

"Two days only." He put on his hat. *Why did men always put on their hat to have the final say?*

"After breakfast——"

"No breakfast. I have to go."

"Very well, Rio. We will prepare food for your journey and bring it to the barn in the morning. Jess will milk Stowe. Faelan will feed the chickens. I will help you feed the stock."

"First light," he said, opening the door.

"First light."

She should be going with him. But he'd hunted alone for many years.

Missouri shivered in the nippy wind and said goodnight.

CHAPTER NINE

Early on November first, the dream came again: *Her parents and Rio rode into the storm to gather the horses, into the thunder and lightning. To save their livelihood, their horses, and for their girls who, all but Faelan, were away finishing their last year at schools, they rode into the rain that pounded into the earth and made it slippery. Heads tucked, they formed jagged images against white flashes.*

I'm coming, *Missouri cried into the darkness.* Wait, Mother, don't go near the edge—

She woke and felt moisture when she rubbed her eyes. "Mama," she murmured, and fought for consciousness.

The rain *dat-datting* on the roof finally roused her. She couldn't have been there to save her parents. But with the bad weather, she should have gone with Rio to find game. She swung her feet over the edge of the featherbed, slipped on a woolen shawl, and went eagerly to the window.

The night was dark as a starling's wing. There was no light in Rio's bunkhouse, no lamp shining from the barn. Panic slid through her.

Forgetting stockings, she slipped into oiled leather boots lined with sheep's wool and hurried out of her room, pounded down the hall, down the stairs. She fumbled with flint. Finally lit two lamps. Grabbing her hat from the hat tree, she flung open the front door, shut it behind her, and carried one of the lamps into a stiff wind, covering the glass to keep the flame. Rain punched with a freezing fist. She gasped and ran through the mud to the bunkhouse.

Inside, no fire. The lamp glow showed the bunk stripped because Rio had taken blankets with him. His bear fur was missing. Above the bed, a calendar from 1885, the year her parents had died, depicted cowboys around a red-gold campfire. The reflected color tinted laughing faces.

The image hurt her. On the trail, Rio had stood well back from the campfires in the midst of the wagons, but he had always looked on, watching. *Longing to be part of the camaraderie? Missing his lost family?* Missouri wished she had made him tell her about his past.

Why were men stoic? So hardheaded and secretive?

Even Rye was closing her out now. It was maddening. Working side-by-side, putting up ropes from the house to the bunkhouse to the barn and the paddock had not thawed his distance.

And now Rio was late. *Lost in the storm, like her parents?*

He had been due back yesterday afternoon. Whether he found game or not, he would never break his word. Never. He was as reliable as night turning to day.

What to do? She couldn't risk her sisters' lives. Go alone to find him? Aunt Gwen's words came to her: *You mustn't live in fear, but you must be prepared for the worst in order to survive.* Could Rio survive out there alone? Could she? Her parents hadn't, and they'd been together. *Dear God*, she prayed. *Keep Rio safe.*

She heard in her memory the wisdom of her Aunt: *Always be with someone you trust.*

She trusted Rye. He was strong and kind and knew

how to ride. She had betrayed her aunt's advice and let Rio go alone, so she must find him and bring him home, and she wanted Rye with her.

Back inside the house, she shouted, "Girls! Get up! Get up!"

Susan came to the dark-wood balcony overlooking the parlor, wrapping herself in a shawl. She leaned over, her braid falling forward, blond wisps framing her face. Voice froggy, she asked, "What is it, Missy? What's amiss?"

"Rio isn't back, Susan. I fear the worst. I have to go and find him."

Her sister turned and ran to Jess's room, rousing her.

Aunt Gwen came to the landing, gray hair frayed. "I heard. I'll get the fire started, and we'll provision you."

"Provisions for three," said Missouri, climbing the stairs, planning the trip. "I'll take Vesta, too."

She didn't say, *In case Rio's mustang is down. In case Rio can no longer ride.*

She'd load the workhorse with food and supplies, an axe, the tent, buckets, the oval tub to water the horses. Vesta could pull a makeshift sled, too, if need be, so Missouri decided to rig the mare as they had done for hauling logs, with driving reins, the singletree, and chains. Just in case.

"You'll get Rye to go?" asked Aunt Gwen, sounding worried.

"Yes."

"You can count on him, dear."

"Yes." Knowing she could was a comfort. She hurried to her room to dress in all the warm clothes she owned.

∽

Missouri, Rye, and the Harper women, even Aunt Gwen, stood just inside the barn. Mugs of coffee steamed. Behind the nutty aroma, horse manure lent an earthy scent, and the chickens clucked and pecked at unseen creatures on the hard-packed dirt floor.

Rain slanted outside the open doors, and inside, the lamps barely raised details from the shadows.

From the foaling stall he shared with Dancy, Traveler whinnied his thin call, and Stowe, tied at the end of the aisle and ready to be milked, bawled and lowered her head to munch hay.

Farm animals could withstand terrible temperatures, but freezing rain could soak them through and cause illness and even death. So they'd brought the animals inside, where they'd been fed and watered.

Missouri turned to Jess. "Fill pails with fresh water for the animals every morning and night. If something happens to that pump—" she gestured to the trough to the left of the barn doors, whose surface ice was melting in the rain "—hitch Betsy to the wagon and take the wagon to the well. Fill the barrels and dispense from them."

"Don't worry," said Jess.

She didn't want the girls battling predators along with sleet and wind. "Keep the animals inside."

"Even the chickens?" asked Faelan.

"Even the chickens."

She turned to their traveling horses, Cricket, Bart, and Vesta. She and Rye wore oversized slickers they'd found in the tack room, the material roomy enough to cover the shoulders and rumps of their mounts.

They'd tied bags and boxes loaded with provisions onto great, gray Vesta and secured a canvas blanket treated with mink oil to shed the rain over the supplies, leaving the ends to protect all but her neck and head.

Vesta stood behind the family, coffee-brown eyes watching the unprecedented gathering of people. Haltered, outfitted, and blanketed, she waited patiently to do her work.

Cricket and Bart were not so docile.

Bart sniffed Cricket's neck. They eyed one another.

Cricket stamped as if to draw a line where overtures from stallions were concerned.

Thank God she was not in estrus, thought Missouri, running through a final checklist. She could think of nothing else they needed to pack.

Turning to her baby sister, "Faelan," she said, "you're not to go to school today."

"Aw, Missy…."

Jess squeezed Missouri's hand and gave her a hug, stepping back with a gleam of moisture in her eyes.

"Now, Jess," Missouri chided gently.

Susan went to stand close to Jess, and Aunt Gwen went to her other side. They were a force, the three of them, wisdom, strength, and love binding them, and it eased Missouri's mind.

She and Rye handed over their coffee mugs.

Faelan said glumly, "Can't I go with you, Missy?"

"No, pet. We'll need you to look after the chickens and Aunt Gwen and Cowboy and everyone. All right?"

At such weighty responsibilities, the child brightened. "Okay, Missy. I'll do what you always do. Promise."

"That's my girl."

Missouri swung into the saddle, the poncho crackling and, underneath, her mother's old sheep's skin duster feeling stiff.

Rye went up, too. He checked his wrapped bedroll and belongings, adjusted the covering over Bart's rump, and, lifting the storm lamp he carried, stepped Bart out into the dawn-threaded rain.

"I love you all," said Missouri, looking down. "Take care of each other. We aim to be home tomorrow, maybe late, maybe the next afternoon. Pray for us."

Amid a chorus of adieus, Missouri rode out. Her spirit grim but determined, she tugged Vesta's lead until she heard the mare's ponderous hooves sucking at the mud behind her.

IT TOOK LONGER than Missouri expected to cross the valley. But finally they made it to the pinons and then the ponderosas, which offered some shelter from the driving storm.

They crisscrossed meadows, climbed up and down hills, looking for tracks. They found horse-droppings— impossible to tell how old with the moisture—but the trail was washed clean of hoof prints, so they continued the search, ascending into the lower slopes of the mountains, calling Rio's name, though their voices were dulled by the downpour.

An hour later, the rain eased to a drizzle.

About midday, Rye asked, "Do you want to rest?"

"No. Do you?"

He shook his head.

They chewed jerky and went on, another hour, two, calling, and searching the ground for signs of Rio's passage. Flakes began to sprinkle down. More than a mile off the valley floor, they found a series of hoof prints frozen in the dirt, heading east.

"His mustang!" Missouri's heart sang. For just this moment, she allowed herself to hope that Rio was alive.

"You sure?"

"See how he wings out on his front feet? That's Rio's horse."

She hustled Cricket and Vesta to a trot and took the lead, heading downhill.

The downy flakes thickened, and her breath clouded in front of her. "Let's hurry," she said, urging the horses. "We'll lose the trail."

"He's heading into that little valley," Rye called from the rear.

She glanced between Cricket's ears and saw a mountain meadow not far below. A pond, iced-up except in the center, was surrounded by frosted cat-o-nine-tails and bushes. It was moose country, and again she experienced a lift in her mood.

When they got to the high meadow, they rode at the edges of the pond, staying out of potentially boggy ground.

The mustang's trail wandered into the trees. Here, Missouri saw where Rio had staked out a spot to wait. Moss was trampled. A horse had trimmed the brush. Above Missouri's head, a branch was broken on some kind of hardwood, leafless and allowing good visibility of the pond. Rio had climbed that tree and watched.

They circled back to the water, and at the eastern shore, in a matted circle of reeds and brush, they saw blood.

Missouri's stomach tightened.

Rye rode off a ways. "Gut pile," he announced. For the first time, he smiled. "He got a moose, Missouri. Early yesterday, by the look of the dried blood."

"But why didn't we find his camp? Why didn't he come home?" She felt tears tighten her eyes, and she held them back. "Where is he?"

"Easy, now. We'll look till we find him." He glanced at the leaden sky. "We might have to make camp though."

"Just an hour more," she said, throat tight. "Please, Rye."

He held her gaze for a moment, and she thought perhaps he was reassessing his coolness to her. "Sure. One hour. Then we make camp."

She wondered what that might mean with regard to the sleeping arrangements. Vesta was carrying only one tent.

But she couldn't think of herself now. She had to find her friend of more than twenty years. Guilt nudged her, but even that she dismissed. Time for regrets later.

"He dragged the moose that way," Rye said, pointing to the mouth of the meadow.

They followed the drag-pattern for two or three miles, out of the valley, down into another, the snow falling faster, the trail getting weaker, the cold nipping Missouri's nose. She snugged her wool scarf over the lower half of her face. Breathing through it, she adjusted to the wet-animal scent and squinted at the broken and crushed vegetation.

"He's heading for our valley," she said, excitement stirring her spirits. "He was coming home."

Ahead of her, Rye nodded. He didn't say, *But why didn't he make it?*

Missouri kept studying the fading signs, as was Rye ahead of her, and she could tell that Rio cut west, skirting the edge of the woods. He would have to. Otherwise, the wide antlers of a moose would catch on every branch and boulder.

They came upon a sparse stand of pinon. The foothills angled uphill on her right. Arroyos angled away to the valley floor. Now, if not for poor visibility, she would be able to see the distant outlines of buildings in Morgan's

Crossing. She was miles from home, but she knew where she was. It felt like a triumph.

"Rye," she called.

He halted and craned around.

"There's a sort of cave."

"Where?"

"Maybe a half-mile ahead, up in those hills."

He turned as though he could see it in the whiteout.

"Keep going," she urged. "We can camp there."

She didn't say what she was thinking: *Rio might be in that cave.* But why would he be? Why not just ride home?

Please be safe, my friend.

Be alive.

As if in reassurance, far ahead, a horse whinnied, muffled by the snowstorm.

Cricket pricked her ears, head canted. She shrilled an answer, and another whinny sounded.

"Rye! Did you hear?"

"I did." And he nudged his stud into a trot, letting the animal pick his way over the covered stones.

If it was possible to fall in love with a horse, Missouri did so now. She gazed in wonder at the shaggy-coated, muscled black body with its beautiful conformation moving against the white prairie—the arched neck set just right above the withers, the ears pricked forward, the nostrils flared, straight slender legs dancing through the drifts.

And the man who sat the stallion so gracefully had his whole heart in her mission. Possibly she was in love with the man, too.

CHAPTER TEN

As he rode along, the snow gathering on Black Bart's mane and the landscape blanketed and silent, Rye wondered how he was going to keep Missouri from suffering horribly if they found her foreman dead. The two were close, as close to family as friends could get.

He'd been feeling that family closeness himself on the evenings and days he'd spent with the Harpers, and it had filled that hole in him that had formed there from his own fool negligence. His sister's face appeared before him, but the memory was so dark he couldn't sustain it.

Instead he thought of Missouri, of his friend Gwenllian, and of the darling Faelan. They were a fine family, the Harpers, well off at one time, refined, caring, educated, hard-working.

And what fortitude Missouri had. What loyalty and courage.

As he rode through the drifts, he shook his head. He'd been a fool, an utter fool to propose courtship. What had he been thinking? He was a liar, a fraud. He didn't deserve her.

But that didn't answer for the loss he felt at not winning her.

Even though he understood her commitment to family and the homesteads, it still hurt to know she'd rejected him, because he admired her so deeply. The veterinarian degree alone amazed him.

Missouri had accomplished a nearly superhuman thing by finishing her degree in the male-dominated profession of animal medicine, let alone at one of the founding universities and vet schools in the country.

The derision and cruel treatment she must have endured from her male colleagues made him seethe when he thought of it. He'd seen the men at his medical school put up signs calling the female students street names, seen them ridicule the women in classes, steal their books, their homework.

He'd gotten into fisticuffs on two occasions. But his interventions had not saved those women their place at his alma mater, nor allowed them to serve humanity as they'd dreamed--a huge waste of talent. Missouri had survived all that.

Thinking of her accomplishments caused him to reflect upon his own choices and feel guilt thread through him. Things were different in his case. He no longer deserved to serve his fellow man—

"Rye," Missouri interrupted. "Turn uphill just after that big pine."

He canted in the saddle. With humor-laced sarcasm, he said, "Yes, dear."

She gave him a crooked grin and waved him off.

He hooked around a giant ponderosa, and Bart lunged uphill. As they went under a laden branch, bushels of white powder dumped on man and horse.

Bart shook like a dog.

They went on, going blindly up with no trail to follow.

Rye had been keeping his distance from the woman he loved and admired. Pride and denial and true feeling for her had prompted him to propose courtship, and after reflection, he knew he shouldn't have. Given his insecurities, she would have come to loathe him, as he loathed himself.

Pride goeth before the fall, he reminded himself. He knew well the meaning of that verse. It could be a deadly thing if ignored. He was definitely fallen.

Beneath the pride was hurt, he knew. His hope to bury his past, make a life with Missouri, to love her and be her husband—his entire scheme for a future here in Morgan's Crossing—had been dashed to bits.

Her refusal left one alternative: find another profession, another life, another small town where he couldn't be found. After placing ligatures on Albert's leg, word might spread about him. Especially since Michael Morgan had witnessed the event.

The worst scenario he could imagine was his family finding him. His mother might write, begging him to return home. He couldn't bear that. He would never again go home.

And now the Harpers would not be his family either. So be it. The pain would eat at him, but he'd endured worse, deserved no less.

"We'll be on our way soon, Bart," he told the horse, and Bart's ears twitched. "Find a new home where there are wide-open spaces. At least that's settled."

Bart snorted, but Rye ignored his retort. His thoughts returned to protecting Missouri if they should find trouble in these woods.

Trouble came soon enough. Ahead loomed an opening between two halves of a mammoth split rock. The russet color of the stone was striking against the clouds of snow, against the green bows with their heavy burdens.

The place was cave-like. A moose carcass hung near the mouth. *Ah no.* Farther into the enclosure, a man's boots. The body lay sprawled and still.

Rio's yellow mustang stood perhaps a half-dozen feet inside the cave, hocks toward the light, its rump torn open and the blood dried to the color of wet bark.

The wounded horse looked around and whinnied piteously.

Cricket answered.

Chilled with horror, Rye swung Bart about on the slope and blocked Missouri's path.

"Don't!" he shouted. "Stay there. There's been trouble."

"What? Is it—*no!*" She unwound Vesta's lead from the saddle horn, kicked her mare, plowed past Rye. She pulled up and leaped from the saddle, pulling her rifle from the scabbard.

And then she saw the shocking scene. "Rio!" she shrieked and ran forward.

Rye shot out of the saddle after her.

HEART IN HER THROAT, Missouri streaked into the cave and hurdled over the body of a dead mountain lion. Throwing down her rifle and eliciting a startled squeal from the injured horse, she crouched over her friend. "Rio!"

He lay face down this side of a grayed-over campfire from which faint heat lifted. His left arm was twisted under him. His head and a shoulder were caked in blood where a patch of his scalp had been ripped open. A glob of red was forming around the gouge in his scalp. *Still bleeding. That meant life.*

Missouri ungloved and felt for the carotid. She couldn't feel a pulse and stilled her breath to try again. *There.* A beat. After a pause, another beat.

Someone nudged her. "Let me," he said.

She fought, realized it was Rye, and said, "Stop. He's alive. I need to—"

"Let me, Missouri," he said. "I know how to help him."

"What? No! Get away. Get my vet kit for me."

She began to turn Rio over.

Rye took her by the shoulders and angled her to look at him. "Missouri, listen. See to the mustang. Let me assess Rio."

Assess. Still in shock, nonetheless she heard the medical term and pulled away, stood up. He had helped that miner. Could she trust him with Rio's life?

Anyway, what did she know about medicine for humans?

Rye opened a leather bag.

She saw what similarly filled her own medical satchel. Rolls of cotton wrapping. Unguents. Bottles of liquid. A stethoscope, which he took out and fitted to his ears. A flask, a wooden box that probably contained syringes, packets of medicines, scissors, pincers, a tiny hammer.

Dizzy with shock and confusion, she staggered toward the mustang. "Pionero," she said in the intonation Rio would use, *pee-o-nero*, trailblazer. "Pionero, stand, now."

The palomino raised his head. His eyes were brown, the whites red-rimmed with stress. He flattened his ears and swished his tail.

"Settle down," she said. The loner man and the loner horse were best friends. "You don't like anybody but Rio. But you're going to have to put up with me for a while."

Deep scratches marred his shoulder. The hide on his upper left thigh had been torn open in a ragged pattern. She went around to his right side. The same shoulder wounds. A set of four punctures on his rear haunch, probably from the claws of the large cat that lay dead near the entrance. The punctures might cause some grief, but she'd clean, disinfect, and leave them to drain and heal.

Touching the artery in his neck, she checked and found the pulse elevated, probably caused by suffering. Pionero would have to endure a bit more, and then he was going to feel a lot better.

After a thorough check, she'd debride the open wounds, trim fouled skin, wash and medicate the injuries, and place loose cotton swatches on the open wounds, letting nature and dressing-changes heal him. Winter was a blessing because flies wouldn't be a problem. The mustang was in his prime. He had an excellent prognosis.

She prayed Rio would make it, too.

With a glance to see that Rye was working on Rio's injuries, she hurried to get her vet bag.

Bart and the other horses were browsing on brush. That would keep them occupied for a while.

After scrubbing her hands in the drifts till her fingers ached, she returned, setting the leather vet kit down on a small rock shelf in the wall near the horse. Opening her case, she took out her stethoscope.

Darkness fell as they finished their medical chores. Missouri watched Rye drag the cougar into the woods to dress it by the light of his outdoor lamp.

Left alone, she gathered the wood Rio had cached and built up the fire. She found his hat in a dim recess and put the hat and his rifle with his poncho, which was folded near his pack.

By reflected glow, she brought the horses into the mouth of the cave and unpacked them, placing Rio's gelding between Bart and the two mares.

Bart, against the wall, raised his head over the mustang's back and checked on his female companions. Evidently he didn't like being separated from them.

Missouri patted his neck. "Leave the girls alone, mister."

Bart snorted.

Pionero ignored his shenanigans.

Tilting the saddles up on their horns and skirts, Missouri laid the bridles nearby, leaving the horses' halters with leads trailing. She removed her slicker so she could move better and tied feedbags on the animals. They began to munch on grain while she thought about supper.

Her stomach grumbled. "I know, I know," she responded. "I'm working on it."

Digging through Rye's food pack, she found basics-- sugar, coffee, and jerky. In Rio's belongings she discovered a skin bag of fat, a pouch of salt, and a small sack of fine-ground cornmeal, his basics for tortillas. From her own pack, she pulled out dried berries, six boiled hen's eggs, a pouch of rice, a couple of strips of dried fish, a bottle of milk carefully wrapped in cloth, and some drying corn-bread they could fry in the grease.

If the weather was bad or Rio hadn't regained consciousness by tomorrow, they had enough food to last for a couple of days. The meat Rye would salvage from the lion would help, too.

From time to time, she checked on Rio, who still slept. Besides several cuts—the bite wound on his scalp being the worst—the lump on his temple worried her the most. She and Rye had concluded Rio was concussed from a fall in the struggle with the cat. The shoulders of his coat had been shredded by raking claws.

She shivered.

Rye had patched Rio's wounds and wrapped him in blankets. Her friend lay near the campfire on the bearskin he'd used as a pallet on the trip west. His dark hair, burnt-sienna skin tone, and high cheekbones made him look Indian.

At least he was untroubled by smoke; it trailed toward the entrance and up between the walls.

Please let him get better, she prayed. *Give him strength.*

The girls would be crushed to lose him, their second father.

Rye apparently knew medicine. She approved of the steps he'd taken to preserve Rio's life.

She thought about her friendship with Rye. If not for worry over Rio, she would have been more able to let go and enjoy this camping trip with him. He seemed to have forgiven her at last. If he wasn't flirting with her anymore, at least he was easy-going, industrious, and a man of good cheer. Best of all, he might have saved Rio's life. It was exciting, really, to be camping with him.

Next to Rio, a tin cup sat on one of the stones that ringed the campfire. The concoction inside gave off herby steam. Rye had her steeping some kind of wild herb, supposed to stimulate Rio's constitution and help him heal.

Rye was a medicine doctor of sorts. Using wild plants for anesthetic and healing remedies combined with traditional medicine for injuries, he seemed to know a great deal. She itched to know how long he'd worked in his uncle's practice and more about his knowledge of plants.

As she waited for him to return, she broadened the base of the fire. Setting the galvanized-steel washtub on hot coals, she filled buckets of snow and dumped them in to melt for the horses. She set rice to simmering, adding the strips of smoked pike from prairie lakes.

Before he left, Rye had asked her to add needles from a white pine outside the entrance to season the rice. "Prevents scurvy," he'd said, smiling as he left. "Makes good tea, too."

So she put on her gloves, gathered some needles, and threw them into the stew.

That done, she looked about their makeshift home and was pleased...and avoided thinking about sleeping arrangements.

Wood would be a problem, though. They had barely enough for a night, and the rest was buried under snow outside. She filled another bucket full of icy white powder, dumped it into the tub, and, leaving the food to steam, grabbed a burning spar and went into the woods to hunt for firewood.

Ice crystals sifted around her, making the torch spit and sputter. With such poor visibility, she stayed near the cave and went around kicking a few mounds. Eventually she was rewarded with odd bits and pieces of pine and pinecones and two heavy spars. She dragged them inside. Hopefully they would dry enough to burn.

Returning from the second trip chilled, she stamped around and slapped her arms, clapped her hands and put them toward the fire. It was blazing now and warmed her.

After checking on Rio, she removed the feedbags from the horses. Going out again, she climbed into the white pine near the cave mouth and tied a rope about ten feet aboveground. She ran the line into the cave, swung up on Cricket, and tied the line high above the horses on a curling root that stuck out of the wall. She ran the horses' lead-lines up and tied them off on the picket line.

She was making a third trip for wood, using her torch, when Rye came through the trees carrying his rifle, the lamp, and a lumpy canvas sack over his shoulder. The slicker billowed, phantom-like. His gloves sprouted out of a pocket, and his hands were rusty with blood.

"Horse killed the cat," he announced, walking toward the cave with Missouri.

"Pionero? Really? How?"

"Teeth and hooves. Ribs were broken. Probably crushed the cat's lungs. I didn't bring the hide because it was torn up, useless for making anything worthwhile but rawhide strings and such."

She shivered. "We have enough to worry about already."

He nodded. "We'll stew the meat if need be. I want to leave that moose cooling till we get home. Butcher it on a clean surface."

"All right. My kitchen or dining room table. How will we get the thing home? It's too stiff to sling over Vesta."

"Build a travois," he said.

He ducked under her sagging tether-line and lugged the meat bag into the cave, where, just inside the mouth, he hung the strings on a rock outcropping. The sack looked insignificant next to the gigantic carcass of the bull moose.

"Something smells good," said Rye, setting his rifle near the fire.

"Pike and rice. A bit of salt."

"And pine needles," he said, sniffing.

"We won't get scurvy," she quipped.

"No, we won't." Chuckling, he collected a bucket and scooped warm water from the galvanized tub. Unwrapping a bar of soap from his pack, he set the bucket against the wall. "Help me with these buttons, will you?" he asked, raising his hands.

She hesitated. Rye could hardly doctor Rio and eat with bloody hands.

His back was to the fire. He turned, waiting.

Tossing aside her gloves, she went to him and unwound his muffler, laying the wool strip on his knapsack. The buttons of his duster were large and easily undone. She stepped away.

"One moment," he said. Balling his hands into fists, he shrugged out of the heavy coat. It fell in a heap.

He wore a shirt the color of wheat, a felt Stetson the color of coal, and the soft leather vest that echoed the hue of his hair. Stubble shadowed his jaw. His eyes, normally blue in the light, looked a mysterious obsidian. "The buttons...can you...?"

She hoped he was wearing long johns under the shirt, as she was.

He wasn't. Bare skin appeared beneath the V of his throat. Keeping her gaze lowered, she opened the buttons, anticipation, however unwelcome, stealing into her thoughts. Missouri told herself she was merely doing a human kindness, keeping him from soiling his clothing with the fluids from gutting the cougar, but undressing him was still unnerving. Steady, she told herself, and slipped loose the last button.

His skin was smooth, the muscle rippling, the scent of his body intoxicating. What would he do if she touched him?

"Go ahead," he said, his voice husky.

She looked into his eyes. "No, I—"

He lowered his head. His mouth claimed hers, gently, sweetly, and she placed her hand on his warm chest and felt the powerful throb of his heart. She'd never been kissed by a man who wanted her. She moved her lips, leaned against him, longing for something within that could only be answered by closeness to him. The lingering, sensuous kiss was unbearably wonderful.

And wrong. So wrong. They were not bound nor promised, and this had been her choice.

She pulled back. "There," she said, voice thready. "Wash, now, and I'll see to Rio and the food."

He touched his hat brim.

She hurried away, listening to the sound of water sloshing.

Why had she kissed him? She knew it was wrong, but the temptation—oh, the sweetness of that kiss. If she'd accepted his suit, she could feel those deep tender feelings and that soft mouth at daybreak and sundown, at midday and midnight. Year after year.

Hands folded across her chest, she closed her eyes and let the vision of valley grasses and big sky, of horses, of mountains, and of this wonderful man, carry her into the future she had forsaken.

HE PRAYED for the distance he needed to endure living closely with Missouri and not take advantage, as he had by kissing her. Though he was not terribly experienced with women—flirtations with San Francisco debutantes aside— he nevertheless instinctively understood that Missouri was untouched and naïve. He had felt a profound tenderness in the kiss, a longing to cherish, to give pleasure, to protect. But following behind the gentleness was passion.

As soon as she'd removed his muffler, he'd felt the need building, and her instincts made her pull back before he took things too far. Just a kiss, he thought. But what a kiss. It had shaken him to his boots. Thank God for the distraction of his patient tonight.

Dressed warmly once more, he glimpsed Missouri, red hair catching the firelight as she pulled the stew from the coals. He whistled inwardly. Even bundled in layers of cotton, wool, and leather, she was a beauty.

And not his. Never his. Because he might turn away at the wrong moment, misdiagnose a stomachache, and their lives would disintegrate.

Let her go. Marriage is not for you.

Rye knelt near the sleeping man.

Rio's face looked ruddy in the firelight. He was regaining health.

Rye put the stethoscope into operation. "Pulse is steadier," he reported, and checked the bandages. "Let's cool that concoction in the cup and see if we can get him to drink some."

Missouri used two sticks to move the tin container away from the coals. Then she came over. "I couldn't imagine life without him," she whispered.

"He's going to make it. He just needs a little time."

"You're sure?"

"No. But I find it helpful to be positive."

She gave him a pat on the shoulder and went back to the campfire.

While he waited for the tea to cool, he watched Missouri double the leather of her long coat and try to lift the tub of melted snow. The water he'd cleaned up in had been just lukewarm. The horses could safely drink what was left in the tub, though the steam rose into Missouri's face.

He reached for the tin cup. "If you'll wait a few minutes, I'll get that for you," he said.

"I can." She put her back into moving the tub, groaning, sloshing water over the rim.

"Maybe not," she said, standing upright and arching her back.

He'd bet she longed to climb into that tub and bathe away her aching muscles.

"Maybe you can do this after all." She grinned.

He smiled.

Turning back to Rio, he lifted him a few inches and tipped warm tea into his mouth. Some dribbled down his chin. Then the swallow-reflex kicked in and some liquid went down Rio's throat.

Across the enclosure, Cricket neighed, asking for a drink.

"Five minutes," Missouri told the mare. "Your water's cooling." To Rye, she said, "Bart is behaving himself."

"He'd better, the clown." At last, he set the cup down and stood. "They eat all right?"

"Every grain."

"Good. I'm famished."

"Me, too."

Rye carried the water tub to the horses, who crowded one another to get the best spot. Slurping and sucking noises filled the cave.

Missouri was reaching for the skillet when Rio moaned. Abandoning the pan, she ran to him.

Rye went to stand beside her.

"*Ay*," said Rio, reaching for the side of his head, the bandage.

"No," said Missouri, gently taking his hand.

"*Ay, me duele.*"

A Californian, Rye understood basic Spanish and recognized "It hurts." The foreman's head and body were going to hurt for a good month at least.

"I know, I know," Missouri said gently, her eyes filling.

Rye put a hand on Missouri's shoulder to steady her.

"I'm sorry I didn't come with you," she said, sounding teary. "I'm so sorry, *mi querido amigo*."

"*No importa*—it's not important. Pionero?"

"He's going to be fine."

"The cat. He is dead?"

"*Sí, esta muerto. Pionero lo mató*—Pionero killed it."

Rye pressed his palm to Rio's forehead. "No fever. Give him more from the cup."

She tipped the liquid into Rio's mouth and he drank. She asked Rio if he could eat rice and fish.

The man shook his head. Lying back, sighing, "*Pionero lo mató*," he closed his eyes.

"Dream well, my friend," whispered Missouri.

Rye, whose stomach rumbled, began serving the food on the tin plates she had warmed.

When they had eaten and checked once more on Rio, Rye sorted out the best sleeping arrangements.

"Let's lie on both sides of Rio." He wished clear to yesterday he could gather Missouri in his arms and hold her all night. "Keep him warm."

"All right."

"I'll cover the three of us with the tent."

"Good idea."

He put a couple of heavy logs onto the coals. Shooting sparks and smoke, they caught, and reflected light flickered on the walls. "That should last an hour or so."

They laid out their bedrolls flanking the sleeping man and, wrapped and covered with every coat and blanket, they climbed into the cocoon, pulling the heavy tent over their heads.

Rye's last thought was a wish to draw Missouri close and cup her face for a goodnight kiss.

CHAPTER ELEVEN

The weather broke cold and overcast, and outside the cave, the drifts rose three feet against tree trunks. Missouri, Rye, and Rio were going home, and she was excited.

While she was scrubbing their dishes next to the morning campfire, across the fire pit, Rio sipped herb tea and watched Rye in the clearing making a litter.

Missouri turned to look.

Bent over parallel bark-stripped poles spaced about four feet apart, the man who had kissed her last night was weaving a hammock with the leather driving reins. A quiver of giddiness went through her. Lord, he looked good, the dark stubble and black hat stark against the snow, his movements supple and his hands quick.

Bart gave a half-whinny. Having eaten and drank first thing, the horses were stamping and snorting and angling to watch Rye, clearly wanting to explore the wonderland they saw. Even Pionero, whom she'd doctored this morning, was mouthing his tether as if to get loose.

Only one thing pulled against Missouri's good spirits--

concern about Rio's head injury, worry that the ride home would injure him more.

Her foreman handed the empty cup across to Missouri to wash. "Pionero *lo mató*, eh?"

"Rye says he killed the lion, yes."

"*Un caballo valiente*—a brave horse."

Missouri agreed.

She listened while he told her he'd reached for his rifle to kill the cat that had come into the cave to take meat from the fresh moose kill. When he moved to shoot the animal, it attacked him, threw him to the floor. He remembered nothing after that.

She nodded and set the tin cup to dry near the coals. "How are you feeling?"

"*Bastante bien.*"

She didn't believe that he felt pretty good. "Your head hurts, doesn't it?"

"*Sí*, a little."

She gave him a wry look. "More than a little, I think."

"I must help him." He gestured toward Rye. "But first...." Rio rolled onto his knees. He panted, then lifted himself to his feet. He swayed.

"No, Rio. You must rest."

Ignoring her, he moved slowly across the uneven dirt floor to Pionero.

The gelding nickered.

Rio explored the chest wounds. He came to the horse's neck and put his good right arm—the left was sprained and in a sling—over the animal's crest. He lay his head against the shaggy neck and crooned.

Missouri saw the mustang lower his head and crane around in the most loving hug between horse and man she'd ever witnessed.

Rye looked up and saw them. Frowning, he dropped the leather straps and hurried between Vesta and Pionero.

The yellow horse pinned back his ears.

"I see you are walking, my friend," said Rye to Rio. "But you must rest while you can. We'll have to ride soon."

"*Sí*, Doctor Rawlins." Rio pronounced it Rawleens "I will rest." He glanced into Rye's face. "You are a doctor, *sí*?"

Rye stared at him for a strange, prolonged moment, then took Rio's arm. "No, no doctor."

"But you fix me."

"Yes, well, I worked for my uncle for many years. He's the doctor. Now, c'mon. Let's get you to bed."

Rye guided Rio to his pallet and eased him onto the bear fur. He covered him and went out without a word.

That was curious, Missouri thought, stacking dishes and pans and carrying them to a box Vesta would haul. She didn't doubt Rye had learned doctoring by assisting in his uncle's practice, but why did he look uncomfortable about it? Or had she misinterpreted the awkward moment?

Rio fell asleep.

Missouri was relieved. She could get the packing done.

Half an hour later, she put on her gloves and went out to Rye. He was crouched over his project, poking pine boughs through the net of reins and rope he'd woven between the poles. Presumably that was to protect the moose hide when it dragged against the ground.

"Looks really good," she said.

"Thanks."

She waited, but he didn't look up nor speak. "Something wrong?"

"No. Nothing wrong. Just anxious to get this done before the snow comes again."

"You want me to get the horses saddled?"

"Yes. But first, hand me the next branch."

She stooped, gave him a scrap of pine. Straightening, she peered at the sky. "Clouds look dark."

"Yeah. We've got maybe an hour. Go ahead and get Vesta's rig on."

"Sure."

She left, a knot forming in her stomach. He'd been companionable if a bit quiet at breakfast. Now he was downright grouchy. What had changed?

Musing upon the mystery, she stood on a bucket to strap on Vesta's harness and hiked onto Cricket's back to untie Vesta's lead. When those tasks were done, she hooked up the singletree and brought the gray out to Rye's work area. "She's ready."

"Do we need to tie her off?"

"She'll stand."

"Okay, back her up to this litter."

"Yes, dear," she said, mocking him from yesterday.

He glanced at her, saw she was teasing. A smile almost surfaced. But not quite.

She lifted the chains and bar, backing Vesta till the singletree was close to the travois.

Rye pulled his skinning knife from one of the poles. "Now you can saddle the others." He leaned to cut rope to tie the singletree to the frame of the litter.

"Before I do…."

Rye looked up, then straightened. He waited, the knife gleaming in his right hand.

"Something seems different with you." She swallowed. "Us."

"There is no *us*, Missouri."

"Oh." She felt the heat climb into her cheeks. "I thought, after last night…."

"You though a kiss would excuse that you refused my suit?"

"No. I mean, yes." She put her gloved hands into her pockets and searched for a way to patch things. "I thought you'd forgiven me, Rye. I want us to be friends."

"I don't want to be *friends*."

A blue jay jeered, and the harsh sound underscored the bleak hurt Missouri felt. Tears tightened her throat. She swallowed them back. After a moment she could speak again. She couldn't ask, What *do* you want? She already knew. "Maybe when we get back—"

"When we get back," he interrupted, sounding angry, "I'm giving my notice to Morgan."

"Notice?" Her heart was pounding.

"I expect to be here only till he can replace me at the mine."

"You mean you're *leaving*?"

"You can't expect me to hang around Morgan's Crossing wishing I could—" he glanced into the trees. Cleared his throat. "Visit you as if nothing has happened between us. Wishing I could—" Muscles worked in his face, and that made her chest ache. "Besides, I've visited too often. People will talk."

"Did they *talk* when you visited Aunt Gwen? She says you came by her cabin almost every day. To check on her, she said."

He shrugged. "Anyway." Then bent to his work.

"Let me worry about idle gossip. The family will be devastated if you leave. You've been the greatest friend to us."

He said no more.

Feeling numb, she returned to the cave. *Rye gone from Morgan's Crossing.* Phrases from that family meeting when Aunt Gwen had admitted how much she missed Uncle

William sifted into her mind. *You live beyond the grief. But you wonder how the days and months go by and you're still breathing without them.*

How would she survive the years ahead without Rye? Her throat closed, and for a moment Missouri couldn't get her breath.

∼

RYE'S GUT WAS RAW. If he had to lie to one more person about his medical skills he was going to scream. Rio was a fine man. He didn't deserve the lies. Missouri and her family and everybody in the area didn't deserve the lies. He didn't deserve their trust. These thoughts churned in him as he rode at the back of the line of horses.

He could hardly wait to start over in some town where nobody knew him. Where there was a doctor to take care of people. And this time he'd ignore cut fingers and sore stomachs and blue eyes with silver arteries in them. He'd refer sick people to the proper medical authorities, because he, for damned sure, wasn't one of them.

The three rode in silence through the thick-falling snow, Missouri ahead on her dun, Rio on his mustang-- moving slowly because both of them were injured--and Rye leading the laden gray who pulled the travois.

He'd had to unhook Vesta from the carrier and drag it close to the moose, then, mounted on Bart, grab the rope, wrap it around his pommel, and ease the moose onto the travois. Finally he'd hooked the workhorse to the litter and dragged the contraption out into the small clearing in front of the cave.

An image of him and Missouri camping alone in that cave tried to wiggle into his consciousness. But disgust at himself kept loving thoughts at bay.

He'd lied to her by omission this morning, making her think his rage was her fault. Now he felt helpless to right things. Instead of explaining, coming clean about being a doctor—about his guilt—feeling trapped, he'd lashed out. What could he do now but ride?

They'd come out of the foothills and were making their way through the pinon pines at the rim of the valley, moving slowly. Obscure light forced them to ride at close range.

Missouri, chin tucked in obvious distress over his rough words, had said she was giving Cricket her head to find the way home. A wise decision. Everything she did was wise.

If he didn't feel so frustrated, he'd be swamped with the anguish of letting her go. *Better to keep the antipathy stirred*, he thought, easing Bart around a lump in the snow that was surely a boulder. *Better to never admit to a soul that Missouri Harper was his one true love, and he didn't deserve to take her to wife.*

Bart danced and pulled at the bit.

"Easy," said Rye, splitting the reins and moving his hands over Bart's withers in case he tried to pull a fast one. His stud had been known to buck when he was fresh. This morning, however, he figured the horse was picking up on Rye's rage.

Rye tried to quell it, to gaze at the valley landscape and lose his anger in the pristine beauty. That didn't work, and Bart danced some more.

Think. Make a plan.

He'd find a place with plenty of people. Living in a small town, he'd found out, made discovery too certain. A city would do.

No, not a city. A thriving town like Morgan's Crossing with grass valleys and rivers full of fish and mountains where you could camp and fill your lungs with piney air. But bigger than Morgan's Crossing. More anonymous.

He'd find a wife and settle down. Have some children.

Absurd, he scoffed. Nobody could measure up to Missouri. Besides, what kind of role model would he be to a family?

Get home, find Morgan. Give him notice.

A plan in place, he set his shoulders and rode toward town.

SNOW WAS STILL FALLING when they got to the barn.

The Harper women crowded around, breath clouding in the freezing air as they helped unload.

Rye felt grateful to be off the range and distracted by the commotion.

Faelan announced the Morgans were hosting a skating party at Silver Lake, east of town, in ten days.

When Missouri asked how she knew, since she was to remain at home, Faelan admitted she'd gone to tell Mrs. Morgan she couldn't teach till the family was reunited.

Rye thought she'd motivated her disobedience rather well.

Missouri let the moment slide without a reprimand.

The child chattered nonstop, hammering the travelers with questions.

Around that sprite Rye found his anger impossible to maintain. He told Faelan the palomino had killed a golden panther and saved his master's life.

Ignoring the gelding's flattened ears, she gave the animal a hug.

The beast tolerated it.

Rio, still mounted, tilted in the saddle, looking exhausted.

The sisters came to a unanimous decision that Rio was to be put on his cot in the kitchen, where they could tend to him and keep him warm.

While Jess helped Missouri clear the tack away from the horses, Susan and Gwen led the mustang across the yard to the side porch and, with Rye's help, eased Rio gently to his feet and into the house.

Rye sat the man on a kitchen chair.

Susan hung Rio's poncho on a hook near the door.

Gwen poured a piping mug of coffee, stirred in honey, and gave the mug to Rio.

He sipped the brew, looking dazed.

Gwen hovered, obviously worried. She didn't need more stress.

"He should be absolutely quiet and in bed for at least a couple of weeks, probably longer," Rye told her.

"I'll see to it." Gwen put a hand on Rio's shoulder, perhaps being protective or to steady him.

Rye wanted to get his stethoscope, but, unwilling to call more attention to his healing skills in front of Susan, he made do with feeling for a temperature—none—and checking his pulse surreptitiously, which was normal.

The man was just wrung out. He'd be in the best of hands with the Harper women nursing him.

In a day or two, Rye would look in on him after he checked on Albert from the mine. They might be the last patients he'd ever tend.

That caused a weightlessness in his gut, and he responded by stepping onto the porch, where he unlaced the rolled bear fur and Rio's pack from Pionero and set them inside the kitchen door.

To Susan he said, "I'll need everybody's help getting the moose into the house. Then I'll bring Rio's bed."

She nodded, let Gwen take over, and went with Rye and the horse to the barn.

They unsaddled the mustang and put him in a stall, and Missouri spent a few minutes re-dressing his wounds.

There was no time to rub down the horses. The light was fading and they needed to get the moose secured. Rye wished he had the strength of Beth Janes here to help.

With the day coming on dusk, Vesta hauled the litter to the front porch. Every last Harper except Gwenllian helped Rye drag the six-hundred-pound carcass into the dining room, where Gwen argued for using the stronger larger table. So chairs were removed, tarps laid, and the great thing lay across the oak table, its antlers gigantic in the room.

Jessamine lit a low fire in the parlor to slowly make the moose malleable to saws and knives the following day.

Rye recommended they keep much of the meat in large chunks that could hang in the barn rafters. "Bar the double doors against predators," he explained, adding that they should ready a rifle and keep it by the parlor door in case a wolf or even a grizzly, late getting into a den, came prowling.

All but Missouri nodded in agreement. She ignored him the entire time.

He worked hard at not resenting her, because her derision was justified.

Next Rye went to fetch the bed from the bunkhouse, where he saw frost on the windowpanes. The iron frame was darned heavy, with mattress springs of twisted coils. Boots squeaking on the dry powder, he humped the cot across the yard, up onto the porch, and into the kitchen. He went back for the ticking.

Gwen made up the cot with fresh linens. Apparently completely taken up with caring for Rio, she asked him no questions about Rye's obviously poor mood.

Feeling he'd eaten glass, Rye returned through the snowstorm to the barn.

Missouri, who kept her chin lifted away from him, and the slender dark-haired Jess, who sent him questioning glances, were nearly done putting Vesta and the others into stalls, watering and graining them.

Bart stood in the aisle munching hay from a hanging wire basket.

The two women made a final trip to a bin at the dim end of the barn, carrying pitchforks full of feed to the horses.

At the other end, the cow lowed, needing to be milked.

Jess sighed, picking up a galvanized bucket.

Rye sidled up to the woman he'd hurt. "Missouri."

She was hanging Cricket's halter on the dividing wall between stalls. She turned, glanced at him. Glanced away.

He took off his hat. "I was rude. I'm sorry."

She gave him a look that was unbending. "I don't forgive you," she said, lifting that lovely chin again.

She went to an alcove and lit a lamp, taking the light to Jess so she could see to milk Stowe. "Be careful carrying the milk to the house," she told her sister. "The snow's getting deep."

Jess had her forehead against the cow's flank and was already drawing milk, the streams *tor-toring* into the pail.

Rye couldn't hear her response.

Missouri came along the aisle toward the barn doors.

"Missouri."

"No, Rye," she said so only he could hear. "You've made it clear you don't want to be my friend. I can never repay you for helping me with Rio, and I'm very, very grateful. I mean that from the bottom of my heart." She made a *mff* sound. "But I'm angry, too. Suddenly you're leaving town? You're like the water faucets in a good hotel. Running hot and cold, depending on…I don't know what. Now, goodnight."

She hurried toward the house, disappearing in the blizzard.

Stung, he walked to Bart and pulled him away from the hay. "C'mon, boy. You're all I have left. Let's get home."

CHAPTER TWELVE

Three days later, the sun shone, and the sky arched over Morgan's Crossing in a blue as deep as on a summer day. But the warmth did not penetrate. Temperatures held at the zero mark. The creek and river froze solid.

Rye, warm-blooded and glad of the cold, which seemed to reflect his bitter mood, nonetheless wore his long johns and a wool sweater under his mining coat for the first time since last winter.

During the hiatus, his penance for incompetence and lies was to miss seeing Missouri. Missing her took the form of a pit of tar in his mid-section.

Working in the mine, where the temperature below-ground read a steady fifty-five degrees, Rye struggled with malaise. He did his job, but he resented every moment spent in the dimness of the underground.

At a lunch break, Bethesda asked him if he was well, and Rye snapped, "Well enough." *For a fraud*, he almost added.

The men steered clear.

Meanwhile, he played cat-and-mouse with Michael

Morgan, to whom he wanted to give his notice. He asked for Morgan at the assay office and was told he'd just missed him. Next day, he went to the man's home, and Mrs. Morgan said he was at the mine. Riding back to the miserable hole in the ground, he learned his boss had gone hunting.

Beth had gone with him. Rye's closest friend going hunting without him felt like a betrayal. That heaped loneliness upon frustration.

Desperate to ease the tension inside, as well as between him and Missouri, on Friday he rode from the mine to the Harper Ranch.

Missouri was out. Perhaps she'd been buying supplies at the company store as he rode past.

After a brief visit with Gwenllian and then another with Rio, Rye was satisfied with the progress of both his patients, although he advised continued bed-rest for the foreman.

Gwen, the only person in town who knew he was a doctor, stepped onto the porch and thanked him heartily for helping Missouri and Rio, and offered a second thanks for his medical advice.

Tipping his hat, he went home to his cabin.

Returning to the Harpers' on foot at dusk the day after, Rye heard Rio's boots crunching on the frozen mud near the water trough. Head bandaged, arm in a sling, the man pumped water into a bucket and carried it to the paddock for the horses' and mules' evening watering.

Speechless with disbelief, Rye spun and strode to the house.

Gwenllian answered the door. "Rye," she said, clutching her wrap and stepping back. "Come in, dear. The kitchen is like Mount Saint Helens in forty-two."

Lord, he was going to miss her warmth, her friendship.

"No, Gwen, I can't. I just wanted to speak to Missouri for a moment."

"Why, yes." She turned to call her niece.

A moment later, Missouri replaced Gwen before him. Dressed in dungarees, boots, and a heavy corduroy coat, the one she used for barn work, she stepped onto the porch.

"Rye," she said, sounding surprised. Then she shuttered the surprise. Her expression grew wary. Reaching back inside, she pulled a battered hat and knitted brown scarf from the hat tree and shut the door. Avoiding eye contact, she took her time wrapping herself and setting the hat over her gleaming red hair. "I was just going out."

Her deliberate slowness infuriated him. He let his breath out in a whoosh. "What in tarnation is Rio doing working?"

She put up a hand to shield her gaze. "What do you mean? Is he all right?"

"No, he's not all right. I just saw him lug a bucket of water for the horses." His tone was harsh, and he let his temper show. "He should be in bed. His head has got to be killing him and his brain requires stillness. Instead, he's doing chores."

Her face whitened. "Not that it's your business."

"I'm his ph—" He caught himself in time, didn't say *physician* "—friend. Any sane person knows a concussion needs rest and quiet."

"I didn't know he—" She did her usual gesture when upset—lifted her chin. "Your tone is unbearably rude, Mr. Rawlins. You think we'd *let* him work? Only this morning I told him he must stay abed. I was going to take care of things."

"Clearly you're not."

"You—you," she sputtered, her cheeks staining pink. "Oh, you hard-headed men."

Firming her mouth, she leaped off the porch and left him standing there, his emotions tumbling.

Realizing he still had the herbs for Rio in his pocket, he had to knock again and give them to Gwenllian.

"Sure you don't want to come in?" she asked, frowning, searching his face for clues to the reason for his hot temper.

"No, no I've got to get back. You feeling all right?"

"Fine, dear. We'll see you tomorrow night."

Miserable and distracted, he saluted and left the porch.

Across the vast yard, Rio was heading for the house or his bunk, head down.

Tomorrow night, if all went the way Rye planned at the skating party with Morgan, he might never visit this ranch again. He was too disgusted to be hurt by the knowledge—mainly with himself.

ON THE MORNING of one of the key social events of the late fall in Morgan's Crossing, the skating party, Rio asked to be moved to the bunkhouse. Missouri tried to dissuade him, but he argued it was too noisy in the kitchen.

He had a point. They cooked and cleaned in the room and held their evening visits. Although he was warm there, the hubbub of the women was too much for a man with a head injury.

So the girls joined forces to lug Rio's bed and belongings to his bachelor quarters. They lit a bold fire and sent the frost melting from the windows, the chill from the dark-pine walls. Lighting a lamp, they set it on the small wooden table near his cot.

With the light and heat, the place became livable,

though Spartan. The only brightness besides the calendar was a serape in reds and blues hanging next to a heavy cotton shirt and a pair of gabardine britches on pegs opposite the stove. Rio wore the serape to ride in summer.

"The place is a bit sad," Missouri observed to her sisters.

Susan shook her head. "We've got to get him some pictures."

"Why not paint him something?" asked Jess.

"Yes," said Susan, "that's what I'll do. Perhaps Aunt Gwen can tat him some doilies."

"I don't think he'd go for fripperies," said Jess, whose tastes ran to simplicity.

Susan and Jess spread the sheets on the cot, followed by Missouri laying out the bear fur.

Once Rio was in his bed, covered with three blankets and the fur, Missouri gave him stern orders to remain there, and she and Susan and Jess went outside.

Her two sisters had agreed to chop wood for Rio's stove. By afternoon they would have stacked enough outside his door on the shallow porch to last three or four days. Meanwhile, Missouri planned to clean the barn, throw down hay from the loft, and tend the animals.

Faelan's shouts brought the sisters running into the yard.

The youngster stood near the far end of the barn, one arm raised and the other wrapped around a pole or a piece of wood.

The mules and horses stared at her from twenty yards away.

"Missy," the child screeched. "Missy, guess what I found?"

"What on earth, Faelan," Missouri demanded,

hurrying across the snow toward her, Jess and Susan close behind.

They arrived huffing white clouds.

"Runners," announced Faelan, grinning. She hauled a rusting length of metal upright beside her. The tip of the runner curved up at the end.

Missouri stuck her fists into her waist. "You scared us half to death."

"Sorry, Missy. But, sisters, there are two of these. We can make a sleigh. Isn't it wonderful?"

The three eldest looked at one another and laughed.

"A sleigh," said Susan, the romantic. "We'll take our sleigh to the skating party tomorrow. It'll be so much more elegant than riding."

Missouri didn't agree—a wagon fitted with rails instead of wheels did not a sleigh make—but she said nothing. "Where did you find them?" she asked.

"At the back of the tool shed. Buried under wire and whatnot."

They kept the wagons, plow, and other equipment and tools in a huge shed behind the barn. The structure was a place of mystery, curious Faelan's favorite place to explore.

Missouri sighed. "Give me a minute to finish mucking the milking area and we'll see what we can do to rasp off the rust and bolt them to the wagon."

Faelan's face bloomed with joy.

If a makeshift sleigh made her family happy, Missouri could ignore the sadness in her heart and cheer them on.

She hadn't even told them Rye was leaving Morgan's Crossing. She couldn't bear to make them cry. When she was in the privacy of her bedroom, her own tears were another matter.

~

AFTER HIS SHIFT at the mine, about dusk, Rye was in his cabin, grinding herbs, imagining cornering Morgan tonight at the skating party, when someone knocked, startling him.

He set the pestle into the mortar, threw on a coat, and, opening the door, stepped adroitly onto the porch, closing it behind him. This was a habit to protect how he lived, surrounded by the clues to a medical past.

The sun had faded. The temperature had dipped to below zero. The air was so still Rye could hear the pigs grunting in Hong Guan's sty, down the road.

A man stood on the shoveled walkway in a hat bespeaking polite society, a felt with a dent in the crown and a narrow curved brim. A beaver overcoat fell to the gentleman's boot-soles, and a pinstriped three-piece suit peeked from beneath the fur. His graying beard was severely trimmed, and a waxed handlebar mustache added a touch of vanity.

A vanity, Rye thought, that reminded him of—

"Joseph!" he burst out, lunging down the step and wrapping his brother in a bear hug.

Returning the hug briefly, Joseph stood back, breath fogging. "Ryenald, my good fellow. Damned cold here in Montana."

Though he loved him, seeing his elder brother was Rye's worst nightmare. Shame flooded him. "Well—well," he stammered. "This is, ah, that is, come in, come in."

The next five minutes were a blur. Full to the brim with joy and regret, he took Joseph's coat and hung it on a peg, sat him in the only chair, served him coffee from a tin pot on the wood stove, and watched him gaze at the ceiling covered with hanging herbs, wild onions, and garlic.

Next his brother peered at the bottles crowded on a shelf above the table—tinctures such as Rye's prized beggar's blanket for bronchitis, tuberculosis, toothache, headache, and cramps—and above, shelves laden with jars of preserved foods.

Disinfected surgery tools gleamed on a white towel on the tiny table. The chamois bag lay nearby, lumpy with implements. Medical books and journals lay staggered along the tabletop.

He watched his brother turn his head. Across the room, Rye's mining coat, grimy and stained, hung on a peg with his other garments.

Rye closed his eyes briefly, feeling trapped—*revealed*.

He rose and fed the stove two chunks of wood, took off his coat, and sat down again, listening to the crackle —*waiting for the condemnation.*

Joseph sipped coffee, gazed again at the ceiling, and said between sips, "Medicine man, are you now?"

"No, it's a hobby. How is…."

"Our mother? You broke her heart. How do you think she is?"

The wound darted through his chest and twisted. He made himself ask, "Pa?"

"Ill."

"*Dear God.* What?"

"Age, I think. Uncle Aedan thinks it's—"

The pause lengthened. His brother took another drink of coffee.

Unable to stand the guilt, Rye snapped, "Go on, say it. I broke his heart, too."

Joseph leveled his gray-blue gaze on Rye. "Yes," he said. "Yes, you broke everybody's heart. Now, come home and fix it."

Rye leaped up. "Are you insane? I can't go home." He swept his arm out to span the humble confines of the cabin and let out another lie. "I have a job, responsibilities. I can't leave."

"Yes, Michael Morgan told me. Seems you have more than mining to do in this, this *hamlet*. You're living a double life, my man."

"I'll never go home," Rye said bitterly.

"Yes, you will."

"You don't understand. I *can't*." Rye sat down. He hung his head.

"We all miss her, you know."

Belle was constantly in his dreams. "Please, brother, could we not speak of her?"

"Eventually—"

"Just not now!" Raw emotion made his voice ragged.

"All right, all right. Calm down."

Rye struggled to regain composure. "How do you know Morgan?"

"We've corresponded. He wrote asking if a man fitting your description was my brother. He already knew about—about Belle." His glance faded away for a moment. "He invited me here."

"For what? To turn the knife?"

"No, brother, to take you home."

Rye shook his head. What was he to do? He longed for home, longed to give his parents the hug of a lifetime. Longed to take Joe to the Harper Ranch and introduce him to the people who'd become his second family—until he'd ruined that, too. *Was there no end to how he destroyed things?*

He considered agreeing to go, then disappearing in one of the rail stops en route to California. He was working out the details when Joseph set his cup down and stood up. "I'll see you tonight for the shindig."

Rye raised his head. "The what?"

"Skating party."

"Oh." It seemed so frivolous, skating when his baby sister would never experience the pleasure of skating on a northern lake in the wilderness.

"The Morgans' invited me," said Joseph, putting on his gloves. "We'll pick you up at six o'clock."

Rye had a million questions—about his brother Teagan, twenty-six now, and Amy, just twenty-one.

But Joe shuffled into his monstrous coat and went out, shutting the door after him.

THE FOOTSTEPS FADED.

Rye sank into the armchair, and a blanket of despair layered over him. He couldn't remember a time he'd been so low. Not since the events three years ago in San Francisco. He felt lost. Adrift.

He couldn't recall Joseph, his idol, ever treating him so condescendingly. Clearly his relatives hated him. Rightfully so. Rye had torn their family apart.

The shock of seeing his brother receded, replaced by the toll of his mistakes. A mistake in judgment, a weakness in his character, a lack of that moral governor--self-knowledge--had cost him everything. Worse, his flaws had cost the family his young sister Belle.

Rye considered saddling Bart and heading out of town. But for the first time, he felt dead inside when he thought of running again.

He'd been a physician and surgeon with a brilliant future.

Who was he now? A liar, a cheat.

If he liked demon rum, he had plenty of cause to kill himself with it, just to make the sadness, the heartache, the losses stop. Rye didn't like rum, but he wanted no more anguish.

Rising from the chair, he searched through his groceries, frantic to find the spirits he used for patients. His *pretend* patients.

Pushing cans aside, hurling them out of the way, he thumped a bag of flour to the floor, where it burst open and showered the planks. He rummaged in an orange crate, looking for the bottle. "Where is it?" he muttered. "Where?"

His head pounded. He put his hands over his ears and tried to stop the throbbing. A part of him knew the pain was psychosomatic, caused by guilt. The images. The memories. *Please stop.* But they would not stop. They came to him clearer and clearer.

His baby sister. Her eleventh birthday. Everyone there, even the governor. Everyone congratulating Rye on his recent medical license.

Belle had come to him complaining of a stomachache, and he, arrogant in his new medical degree, told her to stop eating so much cake. *Stop eating cake! My god, the negligence. With his own flesh and blood.*

He attempted to halt the barrage of recriminations. But they poured ever heavier into his mind.

Run away, the coward in him said. *Hide. Don't let them see you're worthless.* He'd lied to Missouri, to the decent man who ran her place, lied to the town. *Liar, liar, liar.*

Killer.

Rye stopped and looked up, unseeing. Was he a killer?

Certainly he had let his sister die of appendicitis by misreading the signs. Heady with the congratulations of the guests at the birthday party, full of himself, he'd brushed aside Belle's complaints. "Too much cake," he'd told her, raising his glass to a debutante. "Lie down, dear. Let your stomach settle."

147

Then, transparent as a raindrop came the image of her still body on her bed, her face permanently twisted in agony. *God, no.* Futile, his attempts to rouse her, to bring her back.

There is nothing so terrible as realizing your dear one is gone forever. Nothing so soul-tearing as knowing you have the most up-to-date medical knowledge in the world, but it is not enough to bring back the dead.

He wept. He knelt and let out the grief, crying out to the Great Physician for a loving hand. Would he ever be worthy of love?

His sister's young face drifted into his mind. They had adored each other. "Belle," he whispered. "Oh, Belle. Sweet Belle. I killed you, my dearest. I'm sorry, so sorry."

Outside, men's voices. The jingle of harness. Laughter. He didn't care. *Let them come. I'll tell them to go to hell.*

Now he saw Belle as she was before she died, giggling, giving her hiding spot away in their game of hide-in-the-woods. He wanted to hold fast to the image.

A woman's voice drifted to him though the wooden door. His face wet, he gazed at the barrier and thought of Missouri. Once again taking the trust of good people for granted, he'd hurt her. Lied to her. Lovely Missouri. Was it her reliability that drew him when he didn't trust himself?

Yet she was so much more than reliable. She was loving, loyal, hard-working. She was brave. She was full of ambition and kindness.

Unforgiving, too, he reminded himself. *That chin in the air.*

Suddenly he was gripped with the need to see her. He and Bethesda were in charge of organizing the men to put up the tent and set the torches for tonight's event. Surely the Harpers would attend.

Clear-headed and locked on to his moral compass, he

made his plans. He'd go to San Francisco, hug his mother, father, brothers, and sister. Visit his uncle and say he was sorry for letting him down. He would help the family heal. Then he would decide where he and Bart would go next. He held out the possibility of a medical practice but made no decision.

But first he needed to see Missouri. He would not leave until he'd talked to her and made peace.

CHAPTER THIRTEEN

When Missouri arrived at the lake with her sisters and aunt, the cold air hurt her nose and the stars glittered like sapphires. The wind was dead calm.

Not so Missouri's emotions. Her intention was to skate till she was exhausted and at all accounts maintain her poise no matter how unpleasantly a certain dark-haired man conducted himself.

However, if truth be admitted, she wanted to patch their quarrel. She'd behaved badly. Yes, his moods were unpredictable, but that didn't mean she should have rejected his apology and held a grudge.

What if he didn't attend tonight? What if he left without her getting to say she was sorry? That put an ache in her chest, and the ache stayed with her as she surveyed the area.

At the edge of the forest, bathed in moonlight bordering on dusk, a great tent gaped open. Lamp glow spilled over tables of food, chairs scattered about, and a wood stove whose pewter-colored pipe poked through the apex of the tent. A thin stream of smoke rose from the smokestack and disappeared.

Inside the tent, the Morgans, dressed in style, stood next to the wood stove, holding court with some of the townsfolk. Mr. Morgan wore a chocolate brown suit and a long coat. His wife wore a shortened, fitted, lake-blue dress with ermine trim and a matching cape. The outfit looked new.

Barking dogs galloped through a cluster of men in rough clothes who gabbed and passed a cigarette, rifles slung over burly shoulders and holstered revolvers bulging under coats. She saw Bethesda Janes among them.

Two mounted fellows she'd followed on the well-broken trail dismounted and looped their reins over a hitching post behind the tent.

In the shadows among the horses and wagons, the violin player, instrument under his arm, and the scrawny fellow who'd worn the same yellow tie to the dance, were looking over their shoulders and tipping at a canteen.

Around this end of the lake, torches marked the perimeter, kerosene fires wavering over the ice. A few men were skating, bumbling and falling. Their laughter carried to her.

Well done, Mr. and Mrs. Morgan, Missouri thought, appreciating their consideration to the miners and other residents.

As Susan and Jessamine disembarked behind her, boots scraped on the wooden floorboards of the wagon.

Where was Rye?

She sent her gaze over the activity, finally coming to rest on a pair of men under torchlight at the entrance to the pavilion. She must be blinded by her love. He stood right there.

A distinguished-looking man with a handlebar mustache spoke to Rye, but she didn't recognize the stranger. He wore a luxurious fur coat that draped on the snow. In an odd, proprietary gesture, he embraced Rye and went inside to join the Morgans.

When he'd gone, Rye dipped into a wooden crate, lifting out pairs of skates for a huddle of grade-school-aged children.

Cast against the cream-toned canvas, her estranged friend looked dapper in the black Stetson and slim britches. She remembered the kiss, the sweet kiss in the cave, and her responses. She missed him. Why had they fought? It seemed so silly now. His temper. Hers.

Oh my, she sighed inwardly. *How could she possibly let this handsome man leave her?*

"Hello," called Faelan from the side of the wagon, sounding excited.

Missouri turned.

Faelan hopped out. "My students! Hello," she hollered, hurrying to the boys and girls.

When the children saw Faelan, they screamed and jumped up and down, jabbering and clutching her sleeve and pointing to the skate box. Two Oriental boys about thirteen hung back, looking on as if they, too, wanted to join in.

Rye gave Faelan a hug and a pair of skates, which consisted of a blade, a flat bar to rest the foot on, and a leather heel-brace with straps that buckled around the ankle. Rye adjusted the slides that made the skates fit Faelan's boots.

Faelan turned and gestured to the two boys.

Rye got them gear, too.

When she'd run off with her students to sit in the snow and put on the blades, Rye glanced around, apparently searching for someone. His gaze lit on Missouri, sitting on the wagon seat, the reins of the grays lax in her gloved hands.

She held the gaze, and her heart beat far too quickly.

He nodded to her, a slight smile on his lips.

That smile—did it mean…?

A tiny girl at his knee piped a request.

Rye glanced down, smiled, and pulled skates from the box.

The child dashed to Faelan and tugged on her sleeve.

Faelan wrapped the girl in her arms.

Moved, Missouri felt her heart swell with gratitude. For her family. For the Morgans. For Rye.

"What a night," said Susan, standing below the wagon with Jess.

"Isn't it, though," said Aunt Gwen, the girls helping her down from the passenger side of the seat.

They were dressed for the cold. Jess wore men's slacks, a white muffler, and a gray sweater topped by a fitted charcoal-wool jacket from two seasons ago that flared at the hip. The coat was feminine, and her beautiful face and thick dark hair would turn any man's head.

The others wore gowns. Gwen's was a brown wool with a matching heavy-felt cape, carefully mended at the shoulder seam this morning.

Susan was another matter entirely. She had basted her skirts five or six inches higher to avoid tripping. A blue over-long scarf made her eyes vivid, and a royal blue jacket fell to mid-thigh, fitted at the waist and trimmed with fox. The same fur trimmed the muffler, completing an outfit she'd worn on skating outings in their home state. With her flaxen hair spread around her shoulders, she looked stunning.

If Missouri didn't love her so dearly, she'd be consumed by jealousy.

Not that she herself was shabbily dressed. She'd also revived a skating ensemble from years past. Similar to Susan's but of forest green—the neck, wrists, and modified bustle piped in mink—the fitted dress had been cut to calf-length for the sport. She'd left her hair down. Her anxiousness over losing Rye not withstanding, she felt rather attractive in the clothing and looked forward to swooshing over the ice.

Aunt Gwen looked up at her. "Coming, dear? It'll be wonderful fun."

"Yes, I've got to put the horses out back. I'll find you."

"We'll be right here."

She had a good idea where Auntie meant by "here"— with Rye, her best friend.

As Missouri lifted the reins and got Vesta and Betsy going, she wondered how she was going to keep from making a fool of herself over Rye in front of the town.

RYE'S HEART BOOMED. Missouri was here, and he was a new man. He couldn't wait to make things right with her. Although he was leaving for San Francisco as soon as the party was over and Morgan had given him leave, an image kept needling him. Missouri by his side when he returned to San Francisco.

One thing for certain, he wasn't going to be able to practice medicine in Morgan's Crossing. Who would trust him after he'd lied to the people for two years?

Her coming with him was an impossible scheme, and he reminded himself to stick to apologies. But he couldn't quiet his mind and dispel the image of them traveling together. The journey to the mountains had been so sweet. If only she weren't bound to the ranch.

And of course there was Gwen. She was in good hands with the Harper women, eating well and if not strong certainly not as worried and lonesome as before her nieces arrived. But if Missouri left, Gwen, the family, and the ranch might not thrive.

Missouri was the cornerstone. He could hardly woo her away.

Wishing things could be different, he followed her progress as she drove the big work horses behind the canvas.

Gwen and two of her nieces came up to him.

"Rye, dear," said Gwen, moving close and offering her cheek for a kiss. "Isn't it just a perfect night?"

"It certainly is, Gwen." He kissed her and tipped his hat to the sisters. "Ladies, may I get you some skates?"

"Yes," they said together.

He bent to gather two pair for the sisters. In the time he'd known Gwen, she didn't risk falling on the ice.

When he straightened, Susan, looking stunning in fur-trimmed skating clothes, took her pair and said, "You must come with us. Missouri is the best skater in the family. You'll be impressed."

"I'm always impressed by your sister." He scooped up skates for himself and Missouri.

The invitation hadn't come from her. Then again, she hadn't looked away when he'd smiled at her earlier. Maybe they could move about for a while and things would ease enough for him to say his apologies and gain her forgiveness.

At that moment Joseph came to his side. "Morgan would like a word," he said near Rye's ear.

Susan looked up at that moment. Her eyes widened at the sight of Joseph, and her cheeks gained color.

Rye turned to Joseph. His brother looked dazed. He gazed at Susan as if she were Aphrodite. *Goodness, was that attraction blossoming between the gorgeous blonde and his over-serious, work-first bachelor brother?*

"Joseph," he said quickly, before the moment passed. "May I present my dear friend Gwenllian Harper and her nieces Jessamine and Susan. Ladies, my brother Joseph, head of Rawlins Shipping."

His brother nodded to acknowledge Gwen and Jess. His gaze stayed on Susan.

"Listen," said Rye, pleased by the situation because it might bind him closer to Missouri. "I've got to see my boss. Take these." He thrust a pair of size large at Joe. "I was going to escort the ladies around the ice. We can't let them down, can we?"

Before his brother could object, Rye ushered the group to a nearby bench that was a fixture year-round and hurried away.

Inside, the warmth from the stove nearly pushed him over. He'd chopped that pile of firewood against the sidewall, and someone had made liberal use of it. The tent was stifling.

Morgan was deep in conversation with Preston Kincaid, he of the one hundred fifty pounds of oats that had bolstered Missouri's grain stores. They were speaking of new construction and the price of nails.

Rye hovered for a moment, wanting to get his talk with Morgan off his plate, but the men were too engrossed. They didn't even look up.

Prudence Morgan, looking sharp in a blue skating outfit, nodded to him and went back to talking with her plump friend Miss Bertha, something about the price of flour for the boardinghouse.

Morgan's man Howie hovered in the background, seeming to keep a close eye on the new proprietress of the rooming house and its dining area.

Smart move, Rye thought. The man wouldn't go without; Miss Bertha was a fine cook.

With the conversations focused on money, of which he had little, Rye determined he'd have to try again later.

He backed away and was turning toward the open air when he bumped into someone who smelled like spring meadows.

"Oh!" said Missouri, grasping his arms.

Their faces were inches apart. Her lips were rose-hued and looking very kissable. Her eyes were large and dark-blue in the lamplight. "Rye...."

"Missouri," he said quietly. "Beg your pardon."

"No, no, it's my fault." She took a step that felt like a gulf.

Something large and gray sped by behind her, and she began to fall backward. A dog disappeared around the corner.

Rye leaped to catch her. This time he held her close. The scent of meadows filled his head with dreams of possibilities, while his eyes feasted on her pure skin, the wide-set large eyes, the green dress that brought greater contrast to vibrant russet hair.

Her lips parted, and he gathered everything of reserve he could muster to refrain from kissing her. "Seems we're destined to be thrown together," he said softly, searching her face.

She smiled, her gaze full of warmth. "I'm sorry I wouldn't forgive you, Rye. I do. I wanted to say that before you left."

"It's me who should beg your forgiveness. I've been more of a beast than you can imagine."

"Well, you're not a beast to me. You're a hero." She glanced over her shoulder. "Apparently my family has abandoned me. Will you take me skating?"

"Skate with you? Why—" She'd forgiven him! For being mean-spirited but not for the terrible lies he'd told, because she didn't know the truth about him. If he could find a quiet moment tonight, he would tell her everything. Perhaps that would wipe the slate clean with at least one person in Morgan's Crossing. That left the rest of the town. "My pleasure."

Rye reached into the crate, retrieved two sets of rails, and escorted her to the bench.

Missouri took a seat.

"If you'll allow me?" He dropped to one knee, barely feeling the cold snow, extended a hand, and grasped her booted foot.

She gasped. "Well, now you've got it. What can I say?"

Rye laughed, placing the skate against her sole, adjusting the metal, and buckling on the leather strap. Then he did the other foot. Once he strapped on his skates, he stood and offered a hand to Missouri to help her up. For a moment, he looked around to take in the night. Even through the leather glove, he felt the warmth of Missouri's hand in his.

Toward the last torches on his left, Faelan and a gaggle of children giggled and swooped about, falling, and helping each other up.

Out on the ice, his brother skated past, Jess on one arm and Susan on the other, their faces alight with enjoyment.

On the bank several yards away, backed by the dark woods, he saw Beth Janes and Obadiah.

Rye nodded hello and they touched their hats. Other miners standing near his friends saluted.

He couldn't remember when he'd felt so optimistic. He looked down at his companion. "You seem not to care what others think of our friendship. Don't look now, but we've got an audience."

She saw the miners and waved.

All of them waved back and several jostled each other in the ribs.

"Let's give them something to talk about." She squeezed his hand

He and Missouri crossed the snow to the lake. At the edge of the ice, Rye halted. "Obadiah!" he called. "What is that piece of wood under your arm?"

"A violin, a course!"

"Well, let's hear it, then."

The musician wobbled a bit and fitted his instrument under his chin. With a flourish, he set the bow on the strings and began to play a waltz.

They stepped onto the ice. Rye put his arm around Missouri's back and joined their hands in front, enjoying the feel of her body close to his. In seconds they were moving together. It was like dancing on the day they'd met. They partnered perfectly through the long gliding strokes, the turns, the reverses. Susan had been right. Missouri was a wonderful skater.

A feeling of happiness swept through him. His emotions soared. The cold night, the stars, the music floating over the ice to dissipate in the woods, and he and Missouri flowing together—he would remember these moments forever.

On the next violin number, they joined Joseph and the sisters, swirling farther and farther from the torches and closer and closer to the darkness.

Joseph with an uncharacteristic expression of openness locked gazes with Rye and laughed aloud.

Rye hadn't felt close to his brother since Belle died, and the connection tonight opened and warmed his heart. He'd talk to Joe later and make sure they mended their relationship.

Rye felt free. Not since a child had he felt so light, so happy. *If only the pleasure could last with Missouri.*

He let her hands go to skate in circles, and she went opposite, mirroring his moves, her cheeks pink, her lips invitingly ripe for kissing. They approached to complete a figure eight. He leaned toward her. She toward him. Grasping her arms, he swung them and for an instant, their lips met. Sweet, sweet woman.

When Rye straightened, Joseph caught his eye. Eyebrows raised, his brother looked from Missouri to Rye, and then skated away, his arms around the Harper sisters.

The figure eight worked so well Rye decided to do another. He made a great sweeping arc. Leaning forward, hoping for another kiss, out of the corner of his eye he saw a gray blur darting among the trees at the edge of the lake. That dog again.

He did a spiral and flattened out the turn to come close to Missouri.

But the animal shape wasn't right. The creature was too big, and others darted among the pines. A chill went down his back. *The children. Faelan!*

Stopping short, he yelled across the ice. "Beth! Beth Janes. Get your rifle!"

He sprinted past an open-mouthed Missouri toward the far shore.

The children were out there in the near-dark, beyond the torches, Faelan the nearest to the shore.

"Wolf!" he screamed. "Faelan!"

Heart in his throat. Thundering. His breath shortened, his gut tightened, and he balled his hands into fists, skating pell-mell for the shore.

Ahead, the gray shape emerged from the woods, coming for the children. None of them noticed. They frolicked and screamed in play.

Belle's face came to him, that sunny summer morning when he'd found her hiding behind a giant live oak on the family estate. "You found me!" she laughed and darted away.

Then he couldn't bring her back to life, and it had all gone bad.

Not this time, he vowed. *This time she lives.*

Seconds to go.

To his left, a mounted figure coming. A gunshot rang and reverberated.

The wolf left the snow in a mighty leap and grabbed Faelan, shaking her.

Children screamed in terror, running helter-skelter.

Rye, closing the distance with giant strides, flung himself violently at the attacking killer.

He struck with everything in him, all his strength and rage.

The wolf let go of his prey and fell back. Crouching, it turned on him, snarling and slavering, canines gleaming in the wavering light of the torches.

Faelan was down. *Dear god, don't let her die. Not this time.*

Behind him he heard Missouri cry out hoarsely.

"Stay back," he commanded.

The wolf was stalking him, circling, darting glances at the moving figures on the ice. Other shadows wove among the trees, growling.

Rye glimpsed a snow-mounded branch on the bank. He reached, grabbed it, and turned to face the gray beast, wishing he had a tree trunk behind him.

The wolf faded away.

But it came again, locking on Faelan, who was on the ice, squirming, crying. *Alive,* he thought. *But injured. Easy prey.*

Rye brandished the club and screamed, "Here, take

me! Here!"

Turning, the wolf gathered itself, streaked toward him, and launched. Giant jaws. All teeth and red tongue.

Rye put up his left arm, and the teeth sank into his coat and perhaps the flesh beneath. He felt nothing but rage and the will to live.

The attack sent them hard into the snow bank, rolling, the wolf snarling and shaking Rye. The wild, desperate power was like wrestling Zeus.

"Rye!" he heard Missouri scream, but it seemed like a dream. There was only battle. Opening its mouth for a more lethal attack, when the jaws yawned, Rye forced the tree stub into the red mouth. The animal snarled and ripped its head side to side. The stink of canine breath filled Rye's nostrils.

Suddenly the lethal jaws fell away. The animal collapsed, one hundred pounds of dead muscle and bone pressing him down. Only a split second later did he hear the report of the bullet leaving the rifle barrel. He sloughed off the wolf and saw blood pool behind its left shoulder. The lungs or maybe the heart had been hit dead-on.

He turned, saw smoke rising from Bethesda's rifle. He nodded and gulped for air.

Faelan, he remembered, staggering to his feet.

Bethesda hurried over, grasping his arm, searching his face. "You're bleeding, man. Let me—"

"Never mind. I feel nothing. The child. I don't have my medical bag. Ride for it, Beth. It's in my cabin. Gather everything on the table into my leather satchel. Hurry!"

Bethesda ran to the bay gelding standing quivering in the willows near them. His friend was reaching for the reins when Rye shouted, "For the love of god, hurry!"

Hoof beats pounded away.

A crowd closed in, but Rye pushed through them and out onto the ice, still wearing his skates.

Missouri, Susan, and Jess were crouched over Faelan.

Joseph stood a few feet away. "How can I help?"

"Clear off a table in the tent," said Rye, taking sweeping strides to the girl.

"Make room," he said to the women. "I'm a doctor."

The truth had slipped out. The three women looked at him in evident shock. Slowly they rose and stood back.

On his knees, he touched Faelan's neck, checking the pulse. Blood flowed from a cut on the left cheek. He needed more light to check the severity.

"What happened?" Faelan asked. "Am I dead?"

"A wolf got you and shook you but you scared it off," he said, feeling for broken bones in her legs, arms. Taking off her mittens, he found a fracture in the fourth metacarpus on the left hand.

She gasped in pain and tried to pull away.

"You're a warrior princess. They don't mind the court doctor looking them over."

She smiled weakly. "Am I okay, Doctor Rye?"

His eyes burned. What a precious life he held in his hands. "Well, except for that huge stick coming out of your right hand. What is that? Oh. A warrior princess sword."

"It's my skating stick, silly." She giggled, but weakly. "My other hand kind of hurts."

"You don't need the left hand for waving swords, princess. I'm going to pick you up and skate you to your castle. All right? Ready?"

She nodded.

He gathered her against him, cherishing the burden, knowing she wasn't Belle but unable to stop the association. He lifted her, then, nodding to her sisters, and pushed off on his skates, finding a rhythm.

Once inside, where Joseph and a dozen others stood around, Rye laid Faelan on the table. *Where is Beth? Hurry, dammit.* There was no way this child was going to suffer.

"Someone get these skates off of me," he growled, and, as he lifted each foot, Missouri bent down, unbuckled each one, and handed them to someone.

Minutes later, huffing like a hurricane, Beth stormed into the tent. "Your bag, doc."

Rye dug through the contents till he found the pain-killer. He kept the tiny soft balls in a bottle so they wouldn't lose potency. Opening the lid, he dug in, halved a ball, and gave it to Faelan. "Nothing's going to hurt now," he said, keeping his tone gentle.

"Am I going to meet the Frog Prince?"

"Very soon, little one. Very soon."

As he spoke, he checked the cut on her cheek, which required no sutures but needed careful cleaning. When Faelan's eyelids grew heavy, he washed the wound, applied antiseptic powder, and laid a bandage across her cheek.

"Hold this, will you?" he asked Missouri.

She removed her gloves and placed two fingers on the gauze.

"Good," he said, winding cotton cloth from Faelan's chin to her crown to hold the bandage in place. He peeled back two strips at the end of the wrap and tied them.

"Now for her hand." He explained to Missouri, who stood next to him, the damage caused by the wolf. It felt natural to have her support, as if they were medical colleagues, which he guessed they were after the adventures they'd shared.

Drawing a flat piece of alder the length of Faelan's palm from his satchel, he began to bind the wood to the injury.

With his patient out of pain, hand wrapped with sticks

and gauze, satisfaction settled over him. He had doctored Faelan in front of the town, and it felt good. Really good.

Rye finally looked up at the crowd pressing in around him--miners, the sisters, Aunt Gwen, his brother, Kincaid, the Morgans. Confusion on some faces. Surprise on others.

Jess smiled at him. "'Thou art in Rome,'" she quoted.

Indeed, he nearly felt the sand beneath his sandals.

Morgan leaned down and said into Rye's face, so everyone could hear, "You're fired, Rawlins."

Voices combined in a long expression of dismay. This was no crowd in the Coliseum, out for blood. *These were his friends.*

"No, no, I deserve that," Rye said. To Morgan he added, "I was going to give you notice tonight."

"Well, you can't now. I fired you first."

"Fair enough. I want to thank you for two years of work, sir."

Saddened to leave such good people, such a loyal wonderful woman, Rye collected his tools and supplies and repacked them into his medical bag. He glanced up at Missouri.

She looked pale, her eyes worried.

He handed her the bag. "If no one else falls ill tonight, I won't be needing that right away. I'll pick it up in the morning."

She nodded.

"Right after you see me," said Morgan, looking stern. "My home office. Eight o'clock sharp."

"Sir." Rye slid his arms under Faelan's slight body, his own arm where the wolf had clamped down on him aching now.

"Let's get her home," he said to Missouri.

She gazed at him as if he were Washington crossing the Delaware.

CHAPTER FOURTEEN

If it was possible to feel one hundred pounds lighter when you were six-two and healthy, that's how Rye felt, walking down Main Street toward the Morgan home, enjoying the heat wave—ten above zero and rising.

He'd swept out a good deal of his conscience, gotten humble. After the events at the lake. Rye had apologized and told Joe about the lies, the shame, the grief. Joseph, who possessed a heart bigger than most people in their San Francisco circles realized, forgave him instantly.

Rye had patched Faelan and surprisingly somehow healed a part of himself. Now he was on his way to pick up his pay at Michael Morgan's house and say his good-byes.

The only cloud in his sky was leaving Missouri and her family. Saying his adieus to the Harpers, especially her and Aunt Gwen, was going to tear out his guts.

But he owed his family back in Frisco. He needed to make amends. Then he'd see where he and his four-legged buddy would land next. Wherever he settled, maybe he could write to Missouri, give her time to prove up her ranchland. Yes, that was a good plan.

He didn't have to entirely give up hope of being with her. He'd see how things developed long-term.

Rye always felt better when he had a plan. Now that he did, possessed of good will, he waved to a couple of miners heading to their labors and stepped onto the Morgans' front porch. He knocked.

Morgan himself answered, looking serious. A tall good-looking man who dressed well, this morning he wore a brown tweed three-piece and a gold fob for his pocket watch. "Come in, Rawlins," he said, stepping back to admit Rye to a vestibule. Opening a set of double doors, Morgan ushered him into the hall.

Once there, Rye saw a wide staircase leading to the second floor. Fifteen feet away through the open dining room archway, he saw his brother and Mrs. Morgan at breakfast.

Joseph turned, raised his eyebrows—a familiar quirk—and gave a pitying smile.

Taking off his hat, Rye grinned and followed Mr. Morgan into the study.

For a man who owned a gold mine and various properties and concerns, the place was austere. A handsome desk stood under the window, a wooden chair wedged into the opening and another against the wall. A wide ledger lay open on the desktop, quills sprouting from a canning glass. A used coffee cup sat next to an inkwell, and a newspaper lay open, apparently being read when Rye knocked.

Bookshelves flanked a hearth crackling with fire. Only a single shelf on each side carried books. *Room to grow*, he thought, envying the man his settled life with a wife he apparently loved.

Rye spread his hands for warmth. A green design in the tiles lining the fireplace reminded him of Missouri's lovely skating outfit and the gown she'd worn to the dance and the mixed-entertainments show. Distracted thinking of her, he read a spine on one of the books, *The Taming of the Shrew*.

Interesting, given what he knew of Mrs. Morgan's sharp tongue. He'd heard she'd laid into the lazy fellow who ran the company store. Good for her. That man needed a talking-to. The place had been the most uninteresting dustbin of a mercantile he'd ever been in before Morgan's wife got hold of it.

He hoped Morgan wasn't thinking of giving him a tongue-lashing. Severance pay and thank yous would be plenty for this morning's meeting. He chomped at the bit to see Missouri.

"Coffee, Rawlins?" asked Morgan.

"No, thank you. I've got another engagement, then I've got to get packed."

"Miss Harper, I presume?"

Rye jerked his gaze to Morgan's face. He couldn't read the man. "I'm fond of *Mrs.* Harper, too. They're a fine, hard-working family."

"Yes, too bad about Will dying last year."

Wondering where this line of inquiry was going, Rye said nothing.

Morgan drew the chairs around the desk. He gestured, and Rye hung his hat on the ear of the smaller ladder-back and sat down.

Morgan handed him a chamois pouch.

Rye pulled the drawstrings and looked inside. Then he looked again. Gold dust. But far too much for his wages. "But this," he said. "This is wrong, sir. I'm only due ten dollars for the month. Less, because I was short a few days."

Morgan gave a secretive smile. "I have a scheme in mind, Rawlins. I want you to stick around."

"Around, sir? Here?"

"That's right."

"But you fired me."

Morgan leaned back, crossing his arms. "All part of the plan, my good fellow."

Rye scratched his head. "I've got a plan, Mr. Morgan, and it doesn't include staying here in town."

"Oh? Not even for that?" He pointed to the bag of gold.

"What's in here, a hundred? More?"

The man nodded. "One hundred and twenty-nine. I docked you a dollar for the missing days."

"Fair's fair. What would I have to do for that kind of money? You've got a mine foreman. I'm not suited to mine work, anyway."

"But you're suited to doctoring, aren't you, Rawlins?"

A long habit of secrecy made Rye blanche. His recent revelation had been hard-won and hadn't yet sunk in. "At one time I was suited to that, yes."

"Well, how about being my mine doc?"

Shock set in. Faced with the offer, Rye fell back to his old ways. He looked out the window, saw the rustic buildings, a couple of women going about arm-in-arm. "I couldn't, sir. I aim to go back to it, sure, but I—I don't think I'm ready."

"Couldn't prove it by your actions last night."

"Well, it was a simple fracture, a cut, some pretty bad bruises. Nothing you couldn't have done yourself for the child."

A grunt of mirth came out. "Nobody I know besides yourself could have done what you did for Albert Whitney. That cut was deep and lateral. The worst kind. He might have died were it not for you. You'd be a good business investment if you could see your way to saying yes."

169

"I—" This time he choked on the truth, but it had to be told. "My baby sister died because I was negligent, sir. That's why I left my practice at St. Mary's Hospital."

"I know all about it. I wrote to inquire about you."

"And?"

"Received some news accounts along with a written report. Contacted your brother. He vouches for you. Your chief at the hospital called you *gifted*. The business about your sister was tragic, the toughest life-lesson there is. Have you learned from your mistake?"

"Yes. I've suffered and I've learned. I'm a god-fearing man, and I think I can finally make peace with my sister's death." His throat tight, he didn't go on.

"That's good enough for me."

Relief swept him like a stiff wind. Rye held the small pouch of gold in his palm. He'd like to have a ring made for Missouri. If he stayed....

Suddenly a future opened for him laid plumb at his feet. He could earn a decent wage doing the work he loved. And he could see Missouri every week, say he'd wait for her, maybe even win her hand, marry her, someday live at that ranch she'd given her heart and soul to. There wasn't a family in the world, besides his natal family, that he loved more than the Harpers. Would they have him? Would she?

"Mr. Morgan." Rye stood, took his hat. "Thank you for the generous offer."

"Let's make it Michael," he said, also standing. "I wouldn't mind your taking patients in the town when you're not busy with the miners' ills."

"Where would I set up my practice?"

Morgan smiled as if he'd eaten one of the mine canaries. "Got that figured, too. You'll take Gwen Harper's old place, right across from yours. Convenient, eh? With things growing the way they are, why, we might just build you a proper surgery one of these days. Give me a list of your most urgent requirements for equipment and what-not. We'll acquire things a little at a time."

Rye thought over the fundamentals of what he faced as the company physician. "I've only a few concerns."

Morgan looked up. "Oh?"

Rye took a breath and a risk, and said, "I wouldn't be a company man in the usual sense."

"Meaning?"

"Mining is hard, even cruel work. We've been lucky these past two years and there have been relatively few serious injuries. That may change. The standards of safety aren't bad, and thanks to your wife the hours and shifts are more reasonable. However...."

Morgan leaned forward, and Rye knew the timing of his next words was crucial.

"If the men ever sue for wages, safety concerns, or any such item, I will not automatically be a *company* man."

Morgan sat back and studied him. He said nothing for several seconds. "Meaning you will not testify on my behalf?"

"Only if I believe in your case. I'll stand by the side I believe is right."

He picked up a quill and twirled it. "I will admit, that doesn't please me."

"There's more."

"Let's hear it."

"There will be no deduction from the men's pay for my services."

Morgan threw down the quill. "That's outrageous! It's common to deduct the cost of your salary. The boarding house room and board, the meals and cabin or tent rent, the charges to the company store. They're always deducted."

"I know, and the rent is a hardship for the men. They've enough to suffer, Michael. In exchange for your agreement, I'll take less per month, at least for the first year. Shall we say eighty dollars?"

The man let out his breath in a huff. "You drive a damned hard bargain, Rawlins." He put his hands on his knees and, holding Rye's gaze, asked, "Is it a bargain?"

"One thing more."

"Blast!" Morgan shook his head, sighed. "Get on with it."

"I'd like us to get our heads together when the weather's warmer. Think of a plan to deliver the contents of our privies and stables off-site, far from the river. It's thought typhoid is carried in water systems."

Morgan paled. "You mean the river could start an outbreak?"

"Not by itself, no. But if someone out on the plains gets typhoid, and their waste gets into our rivers, it could be deadly for us. Likewise, we don't want to contaminate Silver Lake or the property to the north and east."

"We are expanding," Morgan mused. He took a drink from his coffee cup and made a face. "Anything else?"

"Well, sir, let me get to my other meeting. That will let you think over what I propose, and it'll give me a chance to think on things, too. I'm most grateful for your offer, but a lot depends on—"

"On what Miss Missouri says?"

Rye's face heated to be so transparent that a man he'd been distant with could see his feelings.

"You can't keep courting her like you do," said Morgan with uncanny perception. "Not unless you're promised. In a few months, you could afford to keep a wife."

He'd not keep a wife, not yet, but he sure was going to work on the promise part.

Rye smiled and held out his hand. "Thank you, sir."

"Michael."

"That'll take getting used to. I mean to say, I'm more grateful than I can say to have this fine offer. I will consider it carefully and let you know."

"Shall we say later today?"

"Tomorrow, if that's okay."

"Fine, fine. We'll meet at eight in the morning."

"I'll pick up what's owed me then." Rye set the sack of gold on the desk and nodded to Michael Morgan.

On his way out of the office, Rye turned and caught Joseph watching for him, poking his nose over a newspaper. He gave Joe a thumbs up and hurried outdoors, anxious but hopeful.

CHAPTER FIFTEEN

"Faelan," Missouri said, hanging the dishtowel on a hook and fisting her hands into her waist. "You're not to come to the barn when Mr. Rawlins gets here. All right?"

Her sister pouted. Sitting at the kitchen table, Faelan was jittery as a cricket when the sun was out. Even though deeply bruised on her chest, where the wolf had grasped her jacket and shaken her, and on her arm and hand where he'd bitten her, the pain didn't seem to hold her back. She couldn't sit still.

To keep herself busy on a Sunday with no school, after prayers and reading from the Bible, Missouri had let her borrow some paper from Jess to draw a series of animals that looked vaguely wolf-like, with mountains and a castle in the background. She kept her bandaged hand elevated on the table, per doctor's orders, using her palm to anchor the paper.

"Why can't I go? He'll want to see me, too."

"Yes, he'll want to know how you're doing, and Rio, too. But then Mr. Rawlins and I have some business to discuss and I don't want interruptions."

Faelan looked up slyly and grinned her evil grin. "What kind of business? Love-business?"

Missouri swatted her arm. "Just ask him to come to the barn after he sees to you and Rio."

"Okaaaay." She slumped over her drawing hand and began to pencil in the castle. "But I'm going to serve him coffee first."

"Fine. Now I've got to get some hay down. Don't forget."

Missouri left feeling as nervous as Faelan. Once Rye had gotten her sister situated in the back of the wagon last night, plumping hay to make a nest, he'd taken Missouri aside and said, "I want to talk privately with you tomorrow. Are you willing?"

How could she say no when he had starlight and warmth in his eyes, and he'd just saved her sister's life? "Of course," she'd said. "Of course. And, Rye?"

"Yes, Missouri?"

"You truly are my hero. I will thank you till the end of my days."

"Let's make sure that's at least a hundred years from now."

They'd laughed and sealed the pact with a shake.

Missouri still remembered how safe she'd felt with her hand in his strong and gentle clasp.

BEFORE RETURNING TO THE BARN, Missouri climbed the stairs to change and freshen up. After washing away the dust from her morning chores, she gathered her hair into a fluffy tail and tied it with a red ribbon. She adorned her ears with small gold earrings, a pure extravagance.

It was a work day—every day was a work day—and

she chose freshly washed blue dungarees, fitted more than her other pairs, and tucked in a shirtwaist of red plaid trimmed in tiny white lace. She pulled on the oiled leather boots lined in sheep's wool, her standard for cold weather.

Her toilette complete, Missouri bent to look at herself and determined that she'd done the best she could given she wore no gown. That couldn't be helped. A gown would be ruined in five minutes where she was headed.

Minutes later, high in the loft, breathing the sweet scent of alfalfa, she began scooping hay with a pitchfork and tossing it through an opening in the planks. It landed with a swish in the large bin on the ground floor.

She'd tossed many bunches when she heard the scuff of boots on the dirt below. *Rye?* She told her heart to slow to a normal pace and stepped to the ladder, peeking down.

Grinning as if he'd won a prize, Rye gazed upward.

She hadn't seen him look so happy since, well, since last night, when they were dancing on the ice, laughing like children.

Today for his meeting with Mr. Morgan, he'd dressed in his best off-white shirt, the string tie, and black fitted slacks, Stetson, and boots. No vest, but he wore a blue pullover sweater that matched his eyes, topped with a three-quarter-length charcoal coat of fine wool.

That moment in the cave when she'd touched his bare chest flitted through her mind. She knew full well what fine strong muscles lay beneath the clothing.

Missouri wondered if her appreciation showed in her expression. *Did she care if he noticed? No.* The delight threaded through and through her. She smiled, putting every ounce of gratitude and gladness she was feeling into her expression.

Chuckling, he swung up the steps of the ladder until he stood just below her. "Permission to come board, captain."

"Granted, Doctor Rawlins."

He laughed. "Didn't think I'd like the sound of that."

"But you do now?" She stepped away so he could climb into the loft.

"I think I do. It'll take getting used to."

"You go around saving people day and night. You might as well take credit for it."

"So Rio told me when I spoke to him a while ago." He left that line mysterious and gazed around, taking everything in.

The loft was immense, extending back the length of the barn. The roof slanted to low walls. A mountain of hay rose to the rafters. No light filtered through the roof. Tar felt laid between two crossed layers of planks insulated the walls.

Luckily, although the hay was more than two years old, it remained dry and still had some blue in the flowers. Her small herd could feast on this feed for months to come. With a grain supplement, they should be fine till the spring grass came in.

She and Rye stood on bare boards broken by the entry ladder he'd scaled. In the left corner, a square opened, allowing the hay to be tossed into the box below. In the wall near the bin opening, the exterior haying door showed no light. Sealed and barred, the door could be lifted out on a rope-and-pulley attached to a rafter, and the hay brought in with the haying hook and a horse to pull up the clutch of alfalfa. Her coat hung on the handle of another pitchfork leaning against the eaves.

When he'd finished surveying the barn, Rye turned to Missouri, gazing at her for a long moment that put fluttering wings in her stomach.

"Hello, Missouri," he said, standing so they nearly touched, his gaze full of eagerness and warmth. "You sure

177

are a welcome sight." He pulled a few stems from her hair and tossed them, then ran a forefinger lightly along her chin.

Her knees trembled. "Hello, Rye," she answered. "How—" her voice sounded like a sparrow's and she tried once more "—how did your meeting go?"

"Splendidly. I wanted to go over everything with you."

"By all means." She left him—escaped his male intensity—and took up her coat. "If I'm not moving I'll get chilled."

"Let's finish the hay first," he suggested.

She left the coat and came back, giving him a mock bow. "I'm almost done, but once again I accept your help, sir."

Aware of the how right his presence felt beside her, Missouri showed him how to lift off the edges of hay that were bleached of the green and lay it aside. "That's to cover the floor stalls," she explained. "It's not worth feeding."

He removed his jacket.

He turned his back to remove his jacket, bending to lay it near hers.

Missouri looked her fill at his wide shoulders, marveling at the lines of him, the narrow waist, the muscled haunches. The lines were excellent. Strong, well-defined. A real thoroughbred, was Rye. Maybe half thoroughbred, half quarter—*all that muscle power.*

When he turned back to face her, she glanced at the floor, heat rising into her face.

Rye gave her a curious glance and then dug his fork into the haystack. For five minutes they tossed the good feed down into the bin, the only sounds the swish of the hay.

Suddenly a forkful landed on her head, cascading around her shoulders. With an exclamation, she turned.

Pitchfork thrown aside, he stood a few feet away, his grin challenging, daring her to return the favor.

"On guard," she said, throwing her fork safely out of the way and filling her arms with stall straw. She launched herself at him, the bundle raised over her shoulder.

He dashed to the far wall.

Missouri gave chase.

Rye ducked away.

Again she pursued him, laughing, taunting.

When they reached the middle of the barn, he flung himself backward into the haystack.

She showered him with her armful, the hay landing on his chest.

Chortling, Rye caught her hand and tugged. "Now I've got 'e, cap'n."

She toppled against his chest, both of them laughing.

For a moment Missouri basked in the feeling of her body pressed to his. And then, too soon, she reminded herself this was unseemly, lying atop a man who wasn't her husband. She rolled to her back beside him, breathing heavily and deliriously happy. *Please don't leave*, she longed to say.

Turning, Rye propped his head up and with his free hand traced her chin. "You smell like spring meadows," he said, picking a straw from her hair.

"It's the scent of the hay." She sighed in pleasure.

"No, the fragrance is you." This time when he looked into her eyes, shivers sped through her. Then he heaved a breath of evident impatience. "Now, you know I'm going to San Francisco with Joseph to see the family."

"Oh, Rye, you've ruined a perfectly lovely moment." She started to get up.

He stopped her with his arm across her belly, sending swirling sensations through her, and held her still.

She gazed into his eyes—she never tired of it. "You know you're going to break Aunt Gwen's heart. Faelan's, too." *And mine.*

A spark of excitement lit his eyes. "Only temporarily, my dear. I'm going to be Morgan's mine doctor."

"Really? You're staying? I mean, returning?" What a thrill to know she would not have to say good-bye forever.

"Yes, but first, back to the topic at hand." He plucked more straws from her hair. "Are Gwen and Faelan the only ones who'll miss me?" he drawled. "Hmmm? What about you?"

Now that Missouri couldn't look away, she nodded. "Very well, Ryenald Rawlins of the San Francisco and Washington Rawlinses."

"And the Morgan's Crossing Rawlinses."

"Right. I'll admit, to answer your question, I'll miss you, too. You've been the best friend a woman could—"

"Not just friend," he said softly, running a finger over the lace at her throat. "Isn't that right, Missouri Harper of Missouri and Montana? There's more than friendship here." He stirred his finger in a circle above their bodies. "Lots more."

She regretted firming her tone, but... "I've told you, Rye. I have a family to take care of—"

"Whom I love."

"And two homesteads to prove up."

"Which I'll help you do."

She squirmed around and waited till he saw her serious expression. "I can't marry till I prove up this land."

"I'll wait."

"Quit interrupting. Men always—" She caught her breath. "You'll *what?*"

"Wait till the land is proved up."

Something inside her turned to mush. *Could she possibly have a life with this man she adored?* Missouri had told herself she couldn't for so long she needed time to get used to the idea.

Finally, although she knew what he wanted, Missouri decided she wanted to hear the words. Again. "Why? Why will you wait?"

"Because I want you to be my bride."

She brought her hands to her mouth, barely able to breathe. "Your *bride*," she whispered.

He gathered her against him, snuggling close. "Missouri, I'm willing to wait till you've proved this place" Rye said, his voice husky, intimate. "I believe in your goal, and I love the outdoor life. I'll help you as much as I can when I'm not with patients. I love you, Doctor Missouri Harper, and I'm asking again. May I court you? And when the time is right, will you be my wife?"

"But are you sure? Three years is a terribly long time."

"Do you love me as I love you?"

She closed her eyes for a second to savor her sudden freedom to express her feelings to the man she loved. "Yes," she said fervently. "I love you, Rye. I do."

"Then…?"

"I'd be proud to be your wife, Doctor Rawlins."

"Ha!" He flung one arm out and flopped down. "She loves me. She'll marry me. I'm a doctor again. This is the best day of my life."

She poked him in the ribs. "Silly."

Swift as a cat pouncing on a mouse, he twisted and tickled her ribs. "Call me silly will you." He attacked her once more, making her shriek with laughter.

"Stop," she begged. "I yield. You have the field, sir."

"Thank you, my lovely. Now," he purred close to her

ear, "I have one more question. It's a very important question, perhaps the most important of all."

Something about a ring? A wedding dress? Whether they'd live in the ranch house once they were married? "What is it, my love?"

"I need someone to look after my horse while I'm gone."

"Oh! How to ruin a moment." Giving him a taste of Faelan's evil grin, she said, "Only if I can put him with the mares come spring."

"I wouldn't miss the love-match for the world. I'll be back in a month and we'll make plans."

And he wrapped her in his arms for a proper kiss to seal the bargain.

CHAPTER SIXTEEN

On the sixteenth of November, a gale blew and ice flew sideways, cutting the faces of the Harper sisters as they brought the livestock into the barn to save the animals' legs from being sheared of flesh.

The next day the pitch of the wind rose from a moan to a scream, the snow piled into waist-high drifts, and Missouri reluctantly put on her coat, dreading going outside. Frightened, struggling to stand upright, she felt her way along the ropes to bring Rio firewood and then again to care for the livestock.

Returning to the kitchen with her arms full of wood, Missouri fed the stove and sniffed at the moose roast Susan was preparing for supper. "Smells wonderful."

Susan nodded. "Ready soon."

Aunt Gwen darned a wool stocking by the light of a lamp on the table.

Faelan and Jess were busy mending as well.

The howl of the wind made Missouri shudder, glad to be safe indoors. She hung her coat on a hook.

Aunt Gwen paused her work to sip from a teacup. "Just listen to that gale."

"Good to be inside and cozy." With the wood put away, Missouri washed and dried her hands at the sink. As she often did ever since Rye—with her aunt's reluctant permission—had revealed Aunt Gwen's heart disease, she glanced at her relative. "Have you taken your medicine, Auntie?"

"Yes, dear. And I took a little nap as well."

They were interrupted by the squeak of the door hinges.

In came Rio on a gust of cold air, cheeks burnished. "Ay, dios mio," he murmured, apparently over the weather, and hung his coat over the back of his customary chair. He nodded a greeting, keeping his gaze lowered in his shy way.

Missouri noticed that Aunt Gwen's cheeks pinked, which got Missouri to wondering. *Rio and Aunt Gwen? Why not?*

With all present and accounted for, they took seats around the kitchen table. Susan served the roast, biscuits, and vegetables. When Aunt Gwen said grace, Missouri added a silent prayer that Rye would return safely and in time for Christmas.

As THE MONTH WENT ON, each day Missouri dreamed of the return of her fiancé, but she had to make do with their sparse correspondence. In early December, Bethesda Janes brought one letter from the company store and stayed for supper.

Knowing the family would be anxious to hear his news, Rye wrote so the letter could be read aloud. He described the reunion with his family after two years apart—the joy expressed by his parents, uncle, and sister, and the sadness they felt for his brother Teagan, an attorney widowed at twenty-four.

Rye gave details of the family shipping concern and the wharves and ships and colorful personalities Joseph dealt with at the waterfront. He closed with the words, *Missing you all terribly and praying for your health and happiness.* The letter was signed, *With great affection, Rye.*

No word of his return. No mention of Christmas. That night, Missouri cried alone in her bed.

A second blizzard hit, and, while the snow piled higher and higher and the wind raged, she kept Faelan home. The fourteen-year-old and Rio were nearly healed.

Rye still hadn't returned and now the storm kept him away.

Near Christmas, a thaw gave the residents of Morgan's Crossing hope that a terrible winter would be avoided.

Missouri allowed Rio to resume light duties for half-days.

Meanwhile, she continued the heavy work of the ranch. After moving the stock outside so they could get the sunlight and some exercise, she chopped out the ice in the pasture water trough and lugged numerous buckets to fill the tub, making countless more trips to feed hay on top of the snow.

On Christmas Eve morning, the town gathered at the meeting hall for a celebration. Most conversations revolved around the brutal weather and a delivery of supplies brought in by a local freight-hauler.

Pine bows and red ribbons decorated the hall, and in the humid air, the scents of coffee and stewed foods mingled with musk and the smell of wet wool. Two hat trees by the door held winter coats and scarves.

Missouri and her family wore double sets of long underwear under their dresses and had wrapped in sweaters, knitted hats, and coats to join similarly dressed townsfolk.

The Harper women had prepared two baking sheets piled with strips of moose brisket fried in bacon fat, and as Missouri stood near the stove, missing Rye and watching the moose meat disappear, she felt like crying. But she didn't want to dampen her family's Christmas spirit. They'd been through so much in the past few years and deserved a festive celebration.

She tried to console herself. Perhaps, with the thaw a letter would arrive.

Aunt Gwen moved close and slipped an arm through Missouri's. "Don't fret, dear. He'll come back. He may tell a fib to cover a broken heart, but Rye never breaks his word."

"I know, Auntie, I trust him. I just hope he's well." She smiled down at her tiny relative, then gestured to the table. "Look how the men love that moose."

"Hitting the spot. And Miss Bucholtz's biscuits are disappearing like mice in a tom cat's barn. This is a wonderful place to live, isn't it, dear?"

Missouri hesitated. She wanted to be honest. Yes, she would find moments of happiness with her family and pride in her work at the ranch. But if she had to live without Rye and the hope of their marriage, life would be dark indeed. Then again, living *anywhere* without Rye would be dark.

Before she could answer, the door swung open and Bethesda Janes came in stomping snow from his boots. Immediately the man's gaze sought Jess. Her sister met Beth's gaze and blushed. Oddly, then, Beth turned and stared at the entrance.

Missouri felt envious of the obvious feelings between the two and longed for Rye. No sooner had the thought spent itself than Rye walked through the door. *My dearest love.* Unable to maintain decorum in company, with a huge smile Missouri ran to him. "Rye, *you're here.*" She ran her hands along his arms, feeling the cold fur of his coat under her palms. "*You're safe.*"

He wrapped her in a bear hug and buried his face in her neck. "Missouri," he said, his nose cold against her skin. He raised his head and looked tenderly into her face. "I'm here, my love, and I hope never to leave you again."

She held him, and they rocked a little, a cloud of intimacy surrounding them so that there were only the two of them and the raucous crowd fell away.

"Let me—" he stood back. Tucking gloves into a pocket, he removed his heavy coat, hanging the fur, his black hat, and his scarf on the crowded hat tree.

He looked very fine in his dress clothes, and she wanted nothing more than to snuggle in his arms. But a crowd of men surrounded them, pounding his shoulders and greeting him warmly.

Michael Morgan came over and shook Rye's hand. "Welcome back, Doctor Rawlins. Good to see you."

"Likewise, Michael." Rye grinned, looking young and handsome.

Filled to the brim with gratitude and happiness, Missouri faded to the background, letting him savor the welcome he deserved.

Seconds later she heard him say, "Step back, men. Step back and let me bring the gal I love her Christmas present."

He crossed to her and stood a step away.

Moments later, Missouri saw Prudence Morgan and several women of the town, as well as her sisters, Beth Janes, the miner with the yellow cravat, Mr. Morgan, and others form a circle around herself and Rye.

How unusual to call attention to a gift. What could it be? Her heart began to thud, and her breath shortened in anticipation.

Rye faced her, his expression serious.

She put a hand to her throat. "Rye, whatever…?"

"I told my dear mother about you, Missouri. I told her about your fine qualities and Joseph did, too. I said I wanted to marry you."

The men cheered.

"A wedding!" one shouted. "Let's make it tonight! A Christmas wedding!"

Rye put a hand up. "No, not tonight. She'll need to prove up her land first."

"Awwww," moaned a few, and then silence fell.

"This is a token of my mother's blessing." Rye took something from his pocket. He held it up. The light struck a gold ring with rows of pearls, rubies, and diamonds. "Her own engagement ring."

Missouri drew in an audible breath.

The crowd went "Awwww" again.

"Ain't it purdy?" asked a fellow.

"Sure is," said another.

"Missouri Harper--" Rye held her gaze "--will you wear this ring as a token of my devotion to you and to mark the best years of our lives?"

"I will," she whispered, and he slipped the ring onto her finger.

Cheers went up again

"Kiss her," someone called.

"Kiss, kiss, kiss," they chanted.

As his lips closed over hers, she forgot about the company and put her whole being into expressing her love.

READ ON FOR A SAMPLE OF REBEL LOVE SONG:
HARPER RANCH SERIES BOOK TWO

CHAPTER ONE

Morgan's Crossing, Montana Territory
May 16, 1887

With quick, unladylike strides, Jessamine Harper hurried along the muddy trail leading from the ranch toward Morgan's Crossing. With one hand she carried a tin pan of hot breakfast rolls, and with the other, she bunched up the collar of her wool coat against the cold.

Thank goodness she didn't fit the mold of other women who wore gowns. Gowns were impractical for anywhere but the drawing room, while her trousers kept her legs protected from the chill morning and allowed her to move freely around roots, rocks, and pockets of icy water.

The closer she came to the mining town and seeing Mr. Bethesda Janes before going on to her shift at the mercantile, the more anticipation swirled inside her. With every chance meeting, her attraction to the giant man with a gentle heart grew.

But each time, Jessamine had firmly squashed any

tender emotions, for she had no intention of marrying—at least not until the United States government ratified laws to protect women's inalienable rights. She would not be trapped by convention—her rights, person, property, and future forfeit to the control of a man.

Heat seeped through the cotton cloth Aunt Gwen had wrapped around the tin pan, warming Jess's palm. As she approached the plank bridge over the stream that ran between the Harper Ranch and town, the peeps and whistles of an early robin greeted her. A foot-long patch of snow lay beneath two pines that shaded the bridge, reminding Jess of the winter just finished, the harshest Montana had ever endured in recent history, according to town gossip and articles in the *Billings Dispatch* and the *Great Falls Tribune*.

Millions of cattle had died on the ranges to the north and east, if the reports hadn't been inflated. The Harper women lost two chickens to a January freeze. But the mules and horses, even their cow, had wintered safely in the barn.

Local ranches S Bar D and Circle K lost some animals, but the neighborly spirit of the Morgan's Crossing residents saved many. Bethesda Janes, his best friend Rye "Doc" Rawlins, and other men had gone out in dangerous weather to help cut wire fences, herd the cattle into sheltering arroyos and similar protected areas, and deliver stores of grain and hay to the prairie.

When the mercy missions were over, Mr. Janes and Dr. Rawlins had come with several men to the ranch for supper, the Harpers' contribution to the effort, and they'd reported on the ravaged livestock. Mr. Janes had been well-spoken, as was, of course, Rye Rawlins, educated as a physician.

Jessamine wondered about Mr. Janes' past. During the few times she'd been with him, he'd never spoken of family, of personal interests, of events gone by. He talked of mining, metal-working, the weather, and the animals who'd suffered. Would she eventually discover a mystery in his history? Old pain? Scandal?

Jess shook her head. Seeking truth. Her strength and her Achilles heel. Keeping secret her life's work, her writings, burdened her and sometimes made her restless at night. Unable to tell anyone about her passion, she always had to govern her curious mind and keep from giving away the fact that she processed all she learned with the mind of a journalist-suffragette.

Did her interest in Mr. Janes fit an intellectual category? No, not really, she admitted, her heartbeat quickening.

Passing ragged tents and shanties near the bridge, Jess decided her curiosity about Mr. Janes would overtake her caution if she wasn't careful. Thus, she would draw him out in the future but only for reciprocal kindness. Bethesda had helped her sisters move furniture on two occasions. It was only right she repay his helpfulness with friendliness.

A man emerged from one of the cabins on her left, a clean-shaven miner said to be descended from a Blackfoot warrior. A strip of beaver fur tied back his hair. He wore a slope-brimmed felt hat and a plaid mackinaw and carried a small bucket—presumably his meal.

"Mornin', Miss Harper." He touched his brim.

"Good morning, Mr. George." She nodded.

"The nails I ordered come in yet?"

"Yes, five pounds. Mr. Davis delivered supplies yesterday."

"Thought I saw his rig. I'll be by tomorrow before work."

"Fine. I'll have the chit ready to sign. You can get in and out and not be late."

"Thank you, miss."

She inclined her head.

He hurried east, circling a mounted rider to join a trio of men who emerged from the boarding house and turned right, apparently heading toward the mine.

She'd better catch Mr. Janes before he went to work. Otherwise the yeasty rolls would pass their prime before he could enjoy them.

Arriving at a wrought-iron gate made fanciful by curling vines and leaves, as creative and elegant as ever a gate ought to be, she stepped into a yard sprouting clumps of spring grass. The cabin sat amid clusters of boulders, weathered gray, graced with a sign hanging from the peaked eaves. *Janes Metal Works.*

Now, inside his garden, nerves assailed her. An unmarried female of twenty years risked her reputation by visiting a bachelor at his home. Nonsense, of course. She was not here to seduce him. She'd been sent on a legitimate errand, and she didn't give a fig for the opinions of the townsfolk—except as gossip might affect her family.

The sound of whistling came from the side of the cabin toward the rear.

Jessamine smiled. Mr. Janes was an ace whistler.

She peeked around the wall.

The bearded, powerfully-built miner stood on a stump and reached his mighty arms toward the eaves.

A thousand fluttering wings surged through her. Only relief, Jessamine told herself, because she could talk to him in full public view, scandalizing no one.

He wore a shirt of homespun unbleached cotton— surely size extra-large to accommodate those shoulders— gray gabardine work pants, and sturdy shoes or boots, she couldn't tell which. A thick, trimmed beard the color of black coffee matched the hue of his eyes. The times she'd seen him before, last fall when they'd danced at the town hall and in January and February at the rescuers' dinners, he'd worn his hair parted in the middle and shiny with pomade. When he stopped by the company store on his way to or from the mine, his hair looked pelt-lustrous and natural. More becoming that way, she decided, tamping down her nerves.

A series of peeps came from his hands.

Curious, she walked along the foundation until she stopped a couple of feet from him. She stopped and gazed upward. "Good morning, Mr. Janes."

He stopped whistling and peered down. "Miss Harper —" He sounded surprised, perhaps taken aback, but he went right on with his project, tucking a nest into the eaves.

The peeping grew frantic.

"There, now," he murmured. "Your mama will be back with a worm in three snaps and a flash."

Mr. Janes stepped off the stump, dusted his hands, swept a fall of hair from his eyes, and sniffed the air like a mastiff. "What have you got there, Miss Harper?"

"Some rolls for your breakfast, Mr. Janes." She lifted the towel. Wisps of yeast and flour goodness wafted around them, conjuring warm kitchens and happy families.

Leaning forward, he sniffed again. "They smell wonderful. Did you make them?"

"Aunt Gwen did." She handed the tin to him. "I'm not domestic in the least." She hoped that made her intentions clear against any suppositions he might make. "She said to tell you thank you again for moving the buffet for her."

"No need for that. She already thanked me."

"Just a token of our appreciation, Mr. Janes."

"Why don't you call me Bethesda?" He gave her that warm smile she liked, a smile that said--If you want to be picked up and returned gently to the nest, I'm the man to do it. His smile reminded her of the first day she'd met him, back in September, the night they danced together at the town hall and neither of them could stop smiling.

Smiling and whistling. Good at both. And rescuing birds. What else was he good at? *Making her heart run.*

Gesturing with the tray of rolls, he said, "I'll certainly enjoy these, Miss Harper."

"Call me Jessamine," she said, firming her voice so he wouldn't guess what he did to her. "Or Jess, if you like."

"I'll say…" He deliberated. "Both. Depending on the circumstances."

"What circumstances would those be?"

"Well, for dancing, it would be Jessamine. And if we were out at the lake doing a little fishing, why, I suppose it would be Jess."

Fishing and dancing together sounded nice, she thought wistfully. But such was not to be. At least not the fishing. She couldn't spend time alone with him, become attached. She gave him a polite smile. "Very well, Bethesda. You can decide. Now, I've got to run to the store. Mrs. Morgan expected me five minutes ago."

She whirled, retraced her steps, escaping before he could detect the blush rising in her cheeks.

A WILD PONY galloped beneath Bethesda's ribs. Jessamine Harper did that to him.

A tiny woman with delicate facial features and, he remembered from a dance in the fall, a strong supple body, a light step, and a sweep of wavy black hair a man wanted to bury his face in. These observations teased his senses.

Today she wore all that silkiness knotted at her nape, barely visible beneath the tall collar of her coat. He glimpsed a bit of lace at her throat. She usually wore a white shirtwaist to work, always with britches.

I'm not domestic in the least. He held in a smile. No, perhaps not domestic. Feminine, yes, despite the men's trousers and hat. And beneath those masculine and feminine layers beat the heart of a fighter, he was certain.

He appreciated a woman with spirit. His own mother, though taller, larger-boned, had the mental strength of a field commander—though she lacked enough dominance to overpower the iron will of his father, he reminded himself with a spear of anger. But she had strength enough to manage the pig-headedness of three boys and the independent minds of two girls.

He, Bethesda, would never rule with an iron fist if God blessed him with children. And children he wanted. Children with his strength and Jess's beauty, he mused, watching her walk away. His know-how and her intelligence. The deeper he went into reverie, the deeper the fantasy: *They walked among pines and talked of sculpture, music, the news of the day, the children, the business, chores, financial matters. They laughed and sang together. They leaned close—*

Yes, he concluded abruptly. Jessamine Harper would suit him for a wife. Today wasn't the first time he'd imagined her as a partner. But before any courting could take place, he had to be worthy. Working on it, he told himself. Don't tarry. She'll be snatched up.

As Jessamine neared the far corner of his cabin, he saw her reach into a pocket. Paper crackled. She withdrew an envelope, looked at the piece of mail as if surprised to find it, and returned the letter to the pocket.

Worrisome questions assailed him. Was she writing to a man she cared for back in St. Louis, Missouri--a fellow who had not come west with Jessamine and her sisters last summer? Why would the suitor let them travel alone, without his protection? Why had he not yet arrived to claim her as his wife?

Nonsense. She carried only a shopping list.

Still, he couldn't be sure.

Picking a still-warm roll from the pan, biting, closing his eyes in pleasure, Bethesda munched till the treat evaporated. Then, still thinking about Jessamine, he turned into the shop that connected to his cabin by a back door and went inside, intent on adding some of the fragrant rolls to the canned-venison sandwich he'd wrapped for lunch.

Perhaps Jess wrote to a relative or a friend. Yet surely a lovely young woman like her would have left a few swains bereft when she traveled to Montana.

For the first time since realizing he was interested in Jessamine Harper--that September night at the dance, rather suddenly this morning--Bethesda's feelings deepened. An engine of impatience revved to life inside him. He would need to step up his plans. Otherwise, he might lose his chance with her.

~

To purchase Rebel Love Song, go to: https://montanaskypublishing.com/book-nelson-rebel-love-song.html

A LETTER FROM THE AUTHOR

Dear Reader,

Although I have been writing and publishing for many years, *Rye'sReprieve* is my first published historical novel.

How the novel came about is its own story. My close friend, best-selling author Debra Holland, invited me and several other authors to participate in the launch of her Montana Sky World by writing stories set in the western towns she made popular in her books. So *Rye's Reprieve* was written in 2015-2016 specifically for Debra's Montana Sky World.

You may wonder what qualifies a contemporary writer to publish in historical fiction. In my case, I was raised in rural towns from Northern Maine, where my father was a trapper and guide, to Alaska, where my family fished for salmon and halibut—and the tradition continues with my brothers Dan and John and their sons. Our lifestyle was often exactly like that of a pioneer. I've camped and fished from the East Coast to the West Coast and in Canada, too.

My love of and respect for the natural wonders of America run deep.

If you have suggestions or a few kind words, don't hesitate to write to me through my website, www.LouellaNelson.com, or my Facebook page, https://www.facebook.com/louella.nelson.1. Writers are really encouraged by readers' reviews, so please post your thoughts about *Rye's Reprieve* on the Amazon website. I will notice and appreciate your reactions.

You will find information about my research for this book and my acknowledgements of those many individuals who made this book possible in the pages that follow.

Please enjoy the opening chapter of my next book in the Harper Ranch Series, *Rebel Love Song* (sample chapter), below.

Meanwhile, I can't close without a note of thanks to Debra Holland for her invitation and for mentoring me through the challenges of a Montana Sky World book; to my reviewers, and to my students, many of whom are published and award-winning writers. You give me the confidence to keep on writing.

To my daughter Stacee, thank you for the push to keep publishing. Your inspiration, drive, and love mean the world to me.

Louella Nelson
    Orange County, California

Acknowledgements, Historical Notes, & Quotes for *Rye's Reprieve*

I would like to thank my close friend and colleague Debra Holland for inspiration, for making this novel better by her suggestions, and for the opportunity to write a book set in the world she established through her best-selling Montana Sky series. The setting for my novel, Morgan's Crossing, Montana Territory, was first invented by Debra. In the fall of 2015 and winter of 2016, we spent many hours at my dining table writing together and encouraging one another on our separate projects.

For more on her book titles and background visit her Amazon Author Page at: http://www.DebraHolland.com.

Thanks also go to the wonderful authors who wrote books in her World. We shared historical research, encouragement, and character exchanges so readers could enjoy seeing their favorite characters in other books. To learn about the authors who launched books in Debra's Montana Sky World along with *Rye's Reprieve*, go to her website.

I must thank my copy editor, Adeli Brito of FourEyes-Edit.com, my formatter, Amy Atwell of AuthorEMS.com, both of whom came through for me at the eleventh hour, and my cover artist, Erin Dameron-Hill of EDH Graphics.

In addition, thanks go to Christine Ford, Integrated Resource Program Manager of the Grant-Khor's Ranch in Southwest Montana, now a national park; to Brian Geiger, PhD, MILS, Director, CBSR, University of California, Riverside; to Lori Cassidy and John Dale of Orange Coast College Library; to Erin Eldermire of Vet Library Reference, Cornell University; and to Randy Thompson, Senior Archivist, The National Archives at Riverside, California.

Finally, I would like to thank my cheerleaders: my daughter Stacee Nelson, my sister Grace MacMillan, my nephew and niece Ken and Debbie Rear and niece Shannon Rear, my current students, my former students now published—Alexis Lusonne Montgomery and Janis Thereault—and my dear friend Carl Baggett, Jr.

The lyrics from "It Came Upon the Midnight Clear" that open this novel are attributed in several sources to the Rev. Edmund Hamilton Sears (1810-1876).

The snap fasteners you see on the clothing of the cover model were apparently not in common use for American clothing in 1886 but were patented approximately that year by a German inventor. Other sources suggest the snap was used in stage clothing for quick changes.

"Thou art in Rome" is a quote by Samuel Rogers (1763-1855) that appears in the skating party chapter.

The origins of lyrics from "Blow the Man Down," an English sea shanty, are obscure. The title may refer to the act of knocking a man down. "Contemporary publications and the memories of individuals, in later publications, put the existence of this shanty by the 1860s. The *Syracuse Daily Courier*, July 1867, quoted a lyric from the song, which was said to be used for hauling halyards on a steamship bound from New York to Glasgow." More can be read at https://en.wikipedia.org/wiki/Blow_the_Man_Down.

The most helpful sources for weather conditions and the ravages of the worst winter in Montana history, 1886-1887, can be found at: http://www.nps.gov/grko/learn/historyculture/winter.htm; for a vivid depiction at: http://theweatherforums.com/archive/index.php?/topic/21388-the-winter-of-1886-87-in-montana/; and at: http://www.history.com/this-day-in-history/record-cold-and-snow-decimates-cattle-herds

For sources on the American land grants of the 1880s —most of which conflict as to acreage—which nonetheless are interesting reading, go to: http://history.nd.gov/lincoln/land8.htmlDesert; https://en.wikipedia.org/wiki/Desert_Land_Act; and to pour through the various codes of the Desert Land Act of 1877, which modified the

Homestead Act to allow more land to homesteaders in the west, go to Cornell Law and with great patience consult their archives. Here is a start to your investigation: https://www.law.cornell.edu/uscode/text/43/1303

A non-medical technique for lowering heart rate by massage is found here: http://www.wikihow.com/Slow-Your-Heart-Rate-Down

For early veterinarian practices, see Vets in 1880s: http://www.commercevillagevet.com/historic-hospitals-veterinarians-share-stories-of-three-practices/; although I've owned horses, I needed to reacquaint myself with the parts of a horse and used this site: http://www.dummies.com/how-to/content/identifying-horse-parts-and-markings.html

A truly excellent source for lists of items pioneers often brought with them in wagons crossing the territories is here: http://www.pbs.org/wnet/frontierhouse/images/life_essay2_photo5.gif

I took Rye's middle name from a Civil War hero and claimed the man as his uncle:

John Aaron Rawlins (February 13, 1831 – September 6, 1869) was an officer in the Union Army during the American Civil War. A confidant of Ulysses S. Grant, Rawlins served on Grant's staff throughout the war, rising to the rank of brevet major general, and was Grant's chief defender against allegations of insobriety. After the war, he was appointed Secretary of War when Grant was elected President of the United States, but died of advanced tuberculosis five months into his term. See Chpter 3.

Books I consulted from my library are listed here by title and author and are available currently online:

Days on the Road: Crossing the Plains in 1865, the diary of Sarah Raymond Herndon

Bright Star in the Big Sky by Mary Barmeyer O'Brien

Doc Susie: The True Story of a Country Physician in the Colorado Rockies by Virginia Cornell

Pioneer Doctor: The Story of a Woman's Work by Mari Graña

Doctors of the Old West by Robert F. Karolevitz

Medicine: A History of Healing, Ancient Traditions to Modern Practice, consulting editor Roy Porter (lent to me by Colleen Fliedner, a member of my plot group)

If you would like further information, contact me through my website: www.LouellaNelson.com